Last of the Spirit Seers

Last of the Spirit Seers

Last of the Spirit Seers

Claire Hyatt

THREE CROW Publishing
2014

Copyright © 2014 by Claire Hyatt

All rights reserved. This book or any portion thereof may not be reproduced or used in any manner whatsoever without the express written permission of the publisher except for the use of brief quotations in a book review or scholarly journal.

First Printing: 2014

ISBN 978-1-304-67412-8

Three Crow Publishing
213 Armit Avenue
Fort Frances, ON P9A 2H1

hyatt215@hotmail.com

Book Design by: Claire Hyatt

For Gilbert,
r.i.p

Acknowledgements

I have a list in my head of the many, many people that I have to thank for allowing me this opportunity at such a young age, and I really hope I don't forget anyone important. I am so grateful to everyone for all the encouragement. Most importantly I thank my parents who did so much. They told me I could do it and I did. My mom was my editor and my biggest fan, and my dad had many witty contributions to all of my work. I couldn't have done it without them; they are the reason that it was all possible.

For writing a novel with many true ghost stories that have occurred to my family, friends and to myself, I have many people who contributed to my work; again my parents shared their stories along with my sister Emily, my grandparents, my aunties Tanya and Liana, my cousins Tiana, Caitlin, Sarah, and many others. Without their stories this book couldn't have been possible. I also thank my teachers who encouraged me to keep writing. My soccer, volleyball, and basketball teams and close friends were the ones who always asked me to share all of my ghost stories and to try and pick the scariest one; I have them to thank who inspired me to write a fictional novel about real live paranormal activity.

I'd like to thank Granny and Brian, Hunter, Nik, Aunt Kathy and Uncle Derek who believed in me from the start. Also I really appreciate how my closest friends, Ana, Rachel, Maggie, Anne, Chandler, Max, and Kevin always asked me how my book was going and kept asking for copies; just knowing that people cared about my work really pushed me to try even harder with my book. Oh, and thank you to the many ghosts that I have crossed paths with so far in my life.

Thank you to everyone in my life who has believed in me and told me that I can do anything I set my mind to. I can't believe that my dreams became a reality thanks to all the great people that I know in Fort Frances, Thunder Bay and around the world. This couldn't be possible without all of you. My appreciation also goes out to every single person who purchases and supports my writing. This is my dream come true. I can't thank everyone enough.

Claire Hyatt

Chapter One

They say the eyes are useless when the mind is blind. I stood in front of the big mansion before me. This mansion would be my new home for the next few years. I walked up the long cobblestone pathway closer to the building.

The outside of the mansion was vast and mysterious. Long aging vines stretched up and over the side of the home. I turned around and looked past the gates to take in the beautiful rolling hills that extended on for miles. There were gargoyles greeting me at the top of the corroding stairs surrounded by many bushes of roses. Just beyond the gargoyles was a wooden double door that was pointed at the top. There were silver knockers in the shape of lion's heads, which I used to let my presence be known.

The door slowly creaked open, and I called in to what appeared to be an empty home, "Hello? Is anyone here? My name is Aria Reed."

"Oh yes, Miss Reed. We've been expecting you," a deep voice answered from the shadows. Why my parents had randomly shipped me off to North Yorkshire, England for schooling was beyond me. I had to leave everyone behind, my friends, my siblings and parents, even my goldfish Ralph. I took a step through the door and tried to find the source of the voice.

An old man stepped into view, he was wearing navy overalls full of soot, and he had a long white beard that stretched past his big belly. "I am Mr. Kunkle, the director at this home for the gifted," he piped up, "I believe you will be enjoying your stay here."

"Sir, I don't believe that I am gifted, my parents just wanted me to stay out of all the trouble I was going to get into in Ohio. My grandparents had recommended it years ago."

"Ahh, Miss Reed you are gifted, everyone is in their own way, you just haven't discovered it yet." Mr. Kunkle grinned, "If you don't mind, please follow me to your room."

Claire Hyatt

I followed Mr. Kunkle as well as I could, but this old man had fast legs. Running to catch up I noticed the inside of the mansion. There were beautiful portraits all over the walls, and a long velvet carpet that made its way down every hallway. The floor boards creaked with every step I took. The house had a smell of old books which was overwhelming. It smelled of grass, with a tang of acidity and a hint of vanilla. Mr. Kunkle stopped in front of an old wooden door. The door groaned open and a flow of cold musty air hit my face.

I stepped in to get a load of my room and saw one big cot with purple bed sheets; beautiful purple walls with flowers, and a lovely window seat. The room had a view of the fields beyond the home, and I could see the beautiful red leaves that surrounded the mansion. I turned back to Mr. Kunkle only to realize that he was gone. Where were all the other people, I thought to myself, and what did Mr. Kunkle mean by 'gifted'?

I was bored sitting on my bed waiting for something to happen, and I loved exploring, so I got up to go explore the mansion. Just as I was about to turn the door handle, a knock on the door made me jump a step back. "Uh, come in the door is open." I shouted to the door. I watched the handle turn and in walked two boys. The boys looked very similar, perhaps they are twins.

The two boys exchanged looks. Then the chubbier orange haired boy spoke up, "Hello miss, hehe my name is Gilbert, and this here is my older brother Simon," He spoke in an adorable British accent and his stomach jiggled when he chuckled, "We live here too!"

"Got here a few years back," said Simon the skinnier brown haired boy with glasses.

"My name is Aria, very nice to meet the two of you," I offered a hand.

"Oh the pleasure is all ours miss," the two said in unison. I blushed. After a few hours of chatting about useless information, we decided to go down for dinner.

The dinner hall was stunning and the food was phenomenal. I had wondered where all the other people were, and I must have made it obvious because Gilbert spoke up, "We're the only ones left Aria, the only special kids here, everyone else left..." I sat in silence. Mr. Kunkle gave Gilbert a glare, and so he added, "But that's not important. You don't need to know the background. There are three of us here, and we are going to have a blast." Gilbert beamed. Simon sat poking at his potato salad with a grin on his face.

That night I lay awake wondering of all the secrets those walls held. That's when I heard the noise. Somebody was walking around outside my room. I slowly edged my way to the end of my bed, careful not to make any noise. I slipped on my dog slippers and shuffled toward the door. I barely got to the door when a moan hit my ears and a rush of air knocked me on my rear. I swung around to see a floating girl, her back to me, with flowing hair, and a blood-stained dress. I was petrified. Of course I knew ghosts were real; that is the only explanation to shadows on the walls and whispers when no one was there. But I had never seen one up close in reality.

I forced myself to look back towards the ghost. Bad idea. The ghost was now facing me; I was not prepared for the sight. This tortured soul had no eyes, just empty sockets, and huge cuts that went as deep into her skin as possible. Chunks of flesh were just hanging on by threads. I must have screamed or something because the ghost disappeared when Simon and Gilbert rushed into my room.

Simon returned with a glass of water and Mr. Kunkle as soon as possible. "What the hell was that?!" I finally managed out with a shaky voice.

"That would be your gift," Mr. Kunkle said plainly. A gift? Some gift I have. Oh look how lucky I am, I get to see the dead people all decaying and bloody and shit. How much fun is that! "It is a wonderful gift, and it'll get easier over time Aria, trust me. Just ask Simon or Gilbert"

I look to the brothers with shock. "They have the same gift as me?"

"Yes, we do. And we're a few of the only seers left. Aside from children and animals, there are very seldom who actually have a gift to be able to see the dead." Gilbert shared.

"What good is seeing the dead? It's just traumatizing. Why am I here? My parents sent me for school!" I was so frustrated, and confused. I needed some answers, and soon, just not tonight. I was exhausted and still had jetlag from flying over seas.

Claire Hyatt

Chapter Two

In the morning I was well rested and ready to make people give me some answers. "We'll discuss this during breakfast," Mr. Kunkle had said last night.

I made my way down the grand staircase while I tried to remember my way to the dining room. I was successful in finding the room. Mr. Kunkle sat at the head of the table and looked up at me when I entered the room. Before I had a chance to ask questions, Mr. Kunkle spoke up.

"First things first," Mr. Kunkle started off, "you were sent here by your parents, because we need you. Dark forces are coming and we can't hold them back on our own." I sat and listened in wonder.

"Your grandparents knew me very well when we were younger, they were also seers, and so I contacted your grandparents months back, and they persuaded your parents to let you come." he cleared his throat, " You see, the seeing gift always skips a generation, so it's no surprise you have it, and—"

"My grandparents both died months ago in a car accident." I cut him off.

"Yes, and that is why it was so much more urgent you get here sooner."

I had already eaten all my sausage and was now just picking at the goop my eggs had left on my plate. Gilbert and Simon had taken their plates to the kitchen, and went up to their rooms. It was just me and Mr. Kunkle.

"I don't want to give you too much information to take in right now, so just know, you came here to be safer, and your parents know that. Your grandparents' death was no accident. There are things in this world that you have yet to believe. Now you go wash up, and we'll go for a walk this afternoon."

I rushed upstairs and went to the shower. In the shower I cried. I cried for the death of my grandparents, I cried for the love of my parents, and I cried for what was yet to come. I was afraid.

I began to sing to keep my mind off everything, and halfway through my famous solo, a scream cut me off. I was livid. No one cuts me off during my rock-out to T-swift.

I thought nothing of the scream after my moodiness went away. So I continued on with my song. "CAN'T YOU SEE THAT I'M THE ONE WHO UNDERSTANDS YOU, BEEN HERE ALL ALONG…..WTF." I heard a faint giggle, and then the water got all hot and thick. I looked down at my feet, only I couldn't see my feet. All I could see was red.

It's okay, calm down Aria, it's not real, I tried to tell myself. A bang on the door startled me and I knocked over the shampoo. "Hurry up, you're wasting the day, Kunks is waiting for you!" Gilbert shouted through the door. I guess that was my cue. I hopped out of the shower and threw my long brown hair up into a pony tail.

It wasn't long before Mr. Kunkle came and got me from my room because it was time for our walk. Gilbert insisted he join us on our walk, while Simon chose to stay and read some weird book of his.

We walked out past the gate and towards a row of beautiful trees. This row of trees was actually so perfect, an exact amount of trees on each side of the trail, and not a single branch on the path. "Wow," I exclaimed, "who's your groundskeeper?"

Gilbert laughed, as did Mr. Kunkle. Was there an inside joke I was missing? So I asked again. Laughter arose from the pit of Mr. Kunkle's stomach. "Her," was all Gilbert said pointing to a bench at the end of the trees. There sitting on the white cement bench was a middle-aged woman with brown hair in a bun, wearing a long blue dress.

"That, that, that's a ghost!" I screeched.

"It certainly is; they're everywhere. You never know who's watching," Mr. Kunkle explained. "This particular lady is searching for her husband who left one night and never came home. She froze to death when she got locked in the cellar."

"That's terrible! Did she tell you this?" I was astonished. Mr. Kunkle nodded. "Okay, so tell me, what is this dark force that we are against, and what does it have to do with being a seer?" I still hadn't wrapped my head around the fact that I could see dead people.

"I guess that would be a good place to start. If only I knew." Mr. Kunkle stated. My jaw dropped. "Everyone can see ghosts Miss; it's just based on if you keep your mind open to the possibility that it really is a ghost. Everyone just pushes that possibility away. Once you push it away, it's gone."

He continued, "You don't really get that choice, which is why you are a seer, like us. Your blood-line makes it so that your mind won't shut itself out. You keep all your options open, and look at every angle of a situation."

"That does sound like me. But you're saying you don't even know what the dark thing coming is? I thought you said I was sent here to be safe." Now I was still totally confused with whatever new life was coming to me, yet I was quite interested.

"Someone murdered your grandparents," I suddenly stopped being so chipper with the situation, "there is no easy way to say that, and I am sorry. But the same is happening across the globe. Ghosts are disappearing and being tortured and seers are being killed." Mr. Kunkle spat out. I let a tear slide down my cheek, it landed upon my lips and the taste of salt hit me like a bullet. More tears began coming, and I couldn't stop them.

Why was I crying in public, I never share my feelings? I am supposed to keep those to myself. Mr. Kunkle just let me cry. He gave me a nod, and then he walked back to the house. I sat on the ground in between the rows of trees. I hugged my knees and just sat there. The realization that my loving grandparents had been murdered hit me hard. Did they suffer? Why was it them? I missed them so much.

Gilbert just stood there leaning against a tree watching me, with an apologetic look on his face. The groundskeeper hovered near me holding an old lantern. The tears began slowing down, and I looked up at Gilbert. He was taller than I thought he was, and not nearly as fat. His style was kind of lacking, his clothes were clearly not from this century.

I just sat on the ground. We were both just looking at each other until I stopped crying. Gilbert helped me off the ground and walked me to the house.

"It's coming for us, whatever it is," was all Gilbert said as we walked in silence. I did not want to think of any of this. I had just gotten here yesterday and already my life was being threatened by some unknown killer.

When we got back from our walk it was lunch time. We walked into the dining hall together and greeted Simon. The rest of the day went by very fast. I had not encountered any more ghosts, just the occasional giggle.

The new daily routine was nothing like in Ohio, it felt like all I did was eat and get my brain loaded with information. There was no school; I just studied the past of ghosts. Everyone in the house knew something was coming, but not any time soon, which was a good thing. No one had any idea what it was that was coming, no historical books gave us any information.

I'll admit that I missed my parents at night, a lot. When I used to have terrible nightmares they would always be there to comfort me and tell me that everything was okay and it was just a dream. Now my nightmares were happening when I wasn't dreaming, and they were all real. I'd get to use the old rotary phone, every Sunday to call my parents. I loved the sound of their voices, and it was reassuring to know they were safe. I was glad that I was safe too, for now.

Claire Hyatt

Chapter Three

One morning I awoke from an unsettled sleep just in time for breakfast. By now I had my main routes of the mansion. I sauntered my way down the main hallway to the grand staircase. Crossing one dark hallway I heard a screech. I paused for a moment contemplating my options, I could continue to breakfast and move on with my life, or go check out the strange sound in the creepy hallway. My curiosity got the best of me, and I turned to face the hallway. This hallway was thinner in comparison to all of the other halls in the home. I hadn't ventured to this side of the house yet. Simon was always up for an adventure, but he refused to stray to the north end of the home.

I slowly walked the first few steps down the hallway, but suspense overwhelmed me, and I began to walk faster. I was almost in complete darkness. If I stretched my arms horizontally I could touch the cool walls at my sides. The hallway had no doors, but led towards another hallway. The next hallway was much lighter than the one I was in currently. The screeching continued.

As I neared the next hallway the screeching got louder. A boy came from the left of the next hallway, giggling and facing straight ahead. Trailing behind him was a wooden toy train, attached to an old string he was pulling. Just as the boy was about to go out of sight, the giggling stopped as did the train. I looked up from the train to the boy. He was looking at me. I was startled. I thought to myself, do I say hello? Should I walk away? Is he dangerous?

The boy's face was sunken and his clothes were from the eighteen-hundreds. He had visible scars up and down his arms. I stood there studying the boy as he studied me. I was more startled when he got a big smirk on his face. This was not an 'I'm a cute little boy up to no good' smirk. This was an 'I'm evil, watch your back' smirk.

I took one step back and the boy began to laugh. His giggle was high, and maniacal. I looked into the boy's eyes; he was not nearly as scared as I was. His mouth was open so wide. He continued laughing at me. Bugs began spilling out of his mouth as he laughed. He laughed so hard his skin shook; it shook so hard it began peeling away from his face. I refused to watch anymore of this boy who was falling apart. I turned around and ran.

I ran out of the creepy hallway right down the staircase. I swung on and around the banister in the direction of the dining hall. I must've swung so fast that the banister sent me hurdling into the kitchen, through the swinging door and right into Simon and his plate of flapjacks. I was so embarrassed. I felt my face get red hot as I looked at Simon's syrup covered shirt. "Don't worry about it," he beamed, and blushed back.

Breakfast was plain that day, flapjacks, just like every other morning for the past week. That's what happens when Mr. Kunkle cooks. After breakfast I ran upstairs to get changed, then went down into the library.

The library was my favourite place in the mansion. The old book smell was way stronger in the library, but it added to the effect. This library was just like in the movies. Big tall book cases extending to a very high ceiling, and a ladder that moves along the case. There were many windows in the library, which were always clean. No matter how bright it was that day, the library was always dim and soothing.

This particular morning I was finishing the book 'Where the Red Fern Grows.' I was crying like there was no tomorrow. I'd read the book before, but the ending is always traumatizing. I didn't mind crying in the library, because there was always a feeling of peace. No matter who was in the library, there was always enough room that you wouldn't be very close to anyone. Just as I set the book down, drying my tears, I heard a huge thump at the window. Blood smeared down the window frame and I rose from my seat. I walked towards the window, not thinking that it could all just be in my mind. I looked out the window down into the rose bushes. And sitting right in those bushes was a beautiful crow.

It had hit the window so hard I would've assumed it died on impact, but there it was, moving and cawing. I rushed outside and picked up the bird. The crow tried to peck at me once, but my finger dodged the beak. The crow was too tired and injured to try again, so it gave up and let me carry it inside.

"What are you doing? Get that thing out of my house!" Of course I knew someone would say something. Mr. Kunkle was worried about the crow having diseases and making us all sick. I explained that I had gotten all the bird lice off in the kitchen sink, so the crow was clean.

Gilbert stuck his tongue out in disgust but then chuckled. "I think we should keep it," Gilbert suggested.

"Oh most certainly," Simon agreed, "let's nurse it back to health!" They both seemed really excited over the idea, so I looked to Mr. Kunkle for permission. He nodded.

The three of us ran upstairs like little children to go find a shoe box. By dinner time we had set up a crow sanctuary. I would say that we did a pro job. Not only did we find a shoe box for the crow's bed, but we made a whole house out of cardboard. There was a newspaper for a bathroom and a room for food and water. It was so much fun putting it all together; we had a good time bonding.

During dinner Simon brought up the idea that the bird needed a name. Gilbert and Simon began coming up with ridiculous names like 'Buddy', 'Cupcake', 'Clover', and 'Death.' I sat there laughing. I don't remember the last time

I had laughed so hard. I was enjoying myself, and I had a warm feeling of belonging inside me. The stressful thoughts of murder and ghosts had escaped my mind for the time being.

Mr. Kunkle was very silent and had been sighing at our bird talk all day. I know he wasn't up for the idea of a pet, but I could tell he accepted the fact that we liked it, especially when he offered up a name, "Thorn."

The name immediately stuck, and we knew that was the perfect name. After dinner the three us of quickly ran back upstairs to our new pet, Thorn. Thorn was looking very uncomfortable in the cardboard bed. Simon gladly took up the offer to go get some tea towels for bedding.

When Simon returned he also brought a wooden spoon. Gilbert gave him a quizzical look, and Simon explained, "Kunks told me to bring it for Thorn, that we should use it on her wing and leg so it will heal."

Gilbert snapped the spoon in half and grabbed some string off of my desk to make a splint. Simon held up Thorn as Gilbert set the fracture. I held Thorn's beak as she cawed in pain.

Claire Hyatt

After her injuries were dealt with, we set her down in her comfy bed. Thorn seemed pleased with it.

Chapter Four

A few months passed and the cool winter months were arriving. I woke up one morning and went to look out the window. I stepped over Thorn's sanctuary. I was beginning to think that Thorn was just faking being sick now because she liked the royal treatment.

I walked over to the window and cracked it open a bit. The beautiful red leaves had all fallen to the ground and now left a strong smell of death and decay. If you woke up early enough you could feel the chills that the overnight frost left on the branches.

Every day was a new adventure and I was learning things about seers. Slowly Mr. Kunkle, Simon, Gilbert, and I were learning about this dark force. So far, we hadn't figured out what it and its intentions were, but it was dangerous, and the various ghosts around the mansion knew everything. All the ghosts were reluctant to speak, but eventually we could get it out of them.

I had recently discovered that every soul that stayed on earth after death remained for a reason. The seer's job was to help that lost soul find its way to paradise by fulfilling its task. Simon was very good at speaking with the dead so he taught me how to speak with them myself. My first task with a ghost was the groundskeeper searching for her husband.

I was practically being trained to speak with the dead to prepare myself for whatever was coming. My training was to help find the woman's paradise, whom I met on our walk the first day.

During our many discussions I learned this young lady was named Coraline. Coraline was waiting for her husband to arrive home from war. She planted the row of trees so he'd be able to find his way home.

Coraline froze to death one night after she got locked in the cellar. To this day she still searches for her husband, if you watched out the window late at night you could see her walking around with a lantern searching for her lost love. Coraline's story is a sad unfortunate story. Finding her lover is the key to her paradise.

There was little I could do for Coraline because I don't know where we'd find her husband, and she doesn't even remember his name. He could be long gone. However I wouldn't give up. I refused to let Coraline sit waiting for all of eternity. She was going to have to wait quite a bit though, I had no starting point.

I had stayed up into the late hours watching Coraline and her lantern outside as I sat on the plushy window seat. So I was quite exhausted when Gilbert and Simon woke me up at 6am.

Claire Hyatt

Chapter Five

"Come on, get up Aria!" Gilbert shook me awake.

"You're going to miss all the fun!" Simon exclaimed as he pulled me down the hallway. I struggled to keep up. The boys were so excited about something they sprinted all the way to the kitchen.

Upon stopping in the kitchen, Simon gestured for me to be silent. We stood quietly in the kitchen for a few minutes, and that's when I heard it. Some faint giggling coming from behind the closed door. I looked towards Gilbert and Simon, they were just about ready to jump out of their overalls they were so pumped.

"Well, what do ya say, shall we open it?" Gilbert asked. I was rather excited but a little hesitant. "Come on Aria. What is it you Americans say? YOLO?" I laughed and reached for the door handle.

Just as I was about to turn the handle, the door swung open. A swift giggle in a rush of air passed me and disappeared down the stairs. "To the basement!" Simon exclaimed.

I tried to feel around for a light switch but all I could feel was the cold damp concrete walls. Simon was the bravest when it came to the dead, so he led in front of me, and Gilbert took up the rear.

We took three very slow steps down the stairs before the giggling returned. We were definitely dealing with a young girl. "Come find us, hehehe," whispered the girl.

"We're hiding, find us, find us," came the voice from another young girl. Their whispers gave me chills but we still continued down those creaky old stairs. We safely made it to the bottom of the stairs.

It was pitch black, if I were to hold my hand out in front of my face; I wouldn't even be able to see the outline. Although I couldn't see Gilbert or Simon I could tell where they were standing by feeling their presence in the room. Unfortunately the boys were not the only presence I could feel.

I forgot to put on my slippers when I was awoken, and I could feel the cool wet cement on the floor. The basement had a damp musty smell to it which was very heavy-duty. I began getting dizzy from the strong smells that lingered around us, so I leaned to Simon for support. The three of us leaned on each other back to back.

"We don't want THEM down here," one of the young girls stated, "No boys allowed!" An array of giggles swarmed us, circling the triangle we were in.

Simon tried to reason with them. "We are not here to hurt you, we can help you." Simon spoke very softly and kindly to the girls.

"We know you can't help us, only he can--" something banged somewhere in the distance and cut the girl off. I shivered.

"Who is this 'HE' you are talking about?" Gilbert spoke up. A mean whisper in the coldness stopped the young girl from answering. Simon poked me. Now it was my turn to speak to them.

"What do you want from us?" I questioned quietly.

"You." A very dark deep evil voice spoke. That was our cue, time to get the hell out of that basement. As we ran up the stairs I felt something brush against my neck as the door slammed shut.

"Holy shit, it's locked!" Gilbert shouted as he rattled the door handle. I stared down into the darkness of the basement so freaked out. If I let myself I could've pissed my pants right on the spot. I pictured some evil monster crawling up the stairs like in a horror movie I watched back in Ohio.

"Just do something! We don't know what's down there" I ordered. Gilbert backed up one step and knocked the door down with his foot.

I was so happy to see the sunlight. "I think we just figured out more about that dark force," Simon commented, "We should go tell Kunks about this right away."

If we figured out something about the dark force and it's a man, and those little girls know about him, does that mean he's already been here? I thought to myself. If the evil dark force had been in this house, that could've been his voice in the basement. Does he want me? Why?

Claire Hyatt

Chapter Six

We found Mr. Kunkle in his study talking to the same person he always does, Sampson. Sampson was a blacksmith back in the late seventeen hundreds in North Yorkshire, England. He supplied gun barrels during the American Revolution to the red coats. Sampson had had polio since childhood and so he always walked with a limp and wore leg braces. You could always tell when Sampson was around because you would hear the ka-clinking of his braces.

Sometimes seers get chosen by the spirit and are 'haunted,' Sampson is haunting Mr. Kunkle. Between Coraline and myself, I am not being haunted; I am just helping her out.

Mr. Kunkle told us to go wait in the library for him until he was done talking with Sampson. When Mr. Kunkle walked through the mahogany library doors we all immediately rose from our seats. Mr. Kunkle was very interested in what we had experienced in the basement. He said we might have given him some useful information and so he rushed back to his study.

It was now lunchtime; I had skipped breakfast and was still wearing my pajamas. I thought that it would be a very good idea to make Simon and Gilbert my specialty for lunch, grilled cheese. They loved my meal, despite the fact that I had burned most of the bread. I never was a very good cook. Simon on the other hand was a professional chef; his Cottage Pie was to die for. Made with minced beef and vegetables topped with mashed potato, I could salivate just thinking about it.

I had a very restless night full of nightmares with dead children. The children in my dream all had leg braces on, they marched around me in circles. I couldn't tell if they were young boys or girls because their faces were covered by creepy Paper Mache animal masks. It was one of those anxiety dreams, where you're trying to run to or away from something and finding that you can't move properly, or not at all. My running was slow motion and the children were always around the corner marching towards me.

Claire Hyatt

When I awoke I was in a cold sweat. The thin blankets were not warm enough for the chilly winter months that were coming. I woke at around 5:30am and could not get back to sleep. I threw my hair up into a pony tail and got dressed. After I fed Thorn her corn and apples I looked out the window to see many white puffy flakes of snow falling from the sky. The snow was just settling itself on the ground not making its permanent home there yet. I could see snow across the grounds landing on the rolling hills covering up the browning grass. I stared out the window for a long time watching the sunrise. My breath fogged up the window and I drew the outline of a ghost, I quickly wiped it off and left my bedroom.

I had to be quiet because Gilbert and Simon's rooms were just down the hall from mine and they were still quietly sleeping. I contemplated shaking them awake or throwing water on them, but I wasn't that mean.

I walked down the stairs through the swinging door into the kitchen. Mr. Kunkle must be already awake because the kettle was already heated. I poured the boiled water into a fine china tea cup and added some black tea leaves. While I waited for the tea to steep I took a freshly baked tea biscuit and spread some strawberry jam on it before I devoured it.

When my tea was ready I grabbed a saucer from the cupboard and brought my tea to the library. I sat in the maroon arm chair closest to the window. I sat in the chair sipping my tea until Gilbert came and found me. Gilbert sat in the rocking chair beside me. "The snow came early this year." Gilbert said trying to make conversation. I smiled. "Simon is just in the kitchen fixing us up some breakfast." I loved when Simon made us breakfast because he always made a huge meal, unlike Mr. Kunkle's flapjacks.

Simon called us both to the table half an hour later. His breakfast consisted of fried bacon and egg, mushrooms, sausage, grilled tomatoes, fried bread and of course, black pudding. I ate my whole meal and was terribly full afterwards. During our breakfast, which Mr. Kunkle had missed once again, Gilbert told us about the ghost he was interested in meeting. "I never knew you were haunted! Why didn't you tell us?" Simon had said. Gilbert had explained that he didn't really know if he was being haunted yet, he just saw this quiet ghost every day in the same spot.

Claire Hyatt

The place Gilbert's ghost was seen was walking around outside by the hill in the yard. "Today, let's go find her, and talk to her!" Simon offered. I was down with that plan. I told them that we should watch out Gilbert's window until we saw her.

I sat in Gilbert's window seat until I caught a glimpse of a woman behind a tree. Then the three of us bolted down the stairs to the front door. We put on our shoes and our coats and ran to the front of the house. When I saw this beautiful woman walking towards us she was wearing a very old looking long black dress. She stared straight ahead and walked with such grace. We didn't want to startle her so we walked into her view. It seemed as if this woman was staring straight though us.

It felt as if we were interviewing her when we asked her all sorts of questions. The woman didn't answer any of our questions. However when we brought up this unknown 'HE' that the little girls had mentioned this lady looked right at us. Her face showed fear.

She continued walking our way, yet stayed silent. We backed away when she almost walked right through us.

When she walked further on it was revealed that the back of her dress was a bright red. The tail of her dress dragged in the snow. The lady continued on and then disappeared up over the top of the hill like she has done every day. This lady in red was not going to help us solve our problem. The three of us walked back to the house all rosy cheeked.

 Mr. Kunkle was at lunch and he had made us a ploughman's lunch. Mr. Kunkle was in an awfully chipper mood today. He hummed as he served us our food. After lunch I decided to make a phone call to my parents.

 No matter how many times I'd be taught how to use the rotary phone I still needed help dialing my parents. The overseas extension was too many numbers for me to handle. Mr. Kunkle was busy in his study talking to Sampson so I had Simon do it for me.

 I talked to my parents for a little over an hour. My Mom and Dad were both on the line at the same time so I didn't have to say everything twice. I vaguely explained everything that was going on and how Grandpa and Grandma were not in an accident. The three of us shed tears over the phone and I told them I will make things right. No one was going to murder my loving grandparents and get away with it.

I told my parents about my fears and the experiences I was having. I refrained from telling them about me being seer. I loved my new life, but it was full of danger and I didn't feel that I was ready to face what was coming. I didn't want to be a failure to everyone I loved. I wouldn't fail for Grandma. Then my Mom told me what she had been telling me since I was young, "Glory isn't never falling, but getting back up when you do."

The three of us discussed how the Christmas season was coming up. My parents had a very hard time telling me that they couldn't afford to send me home for the holidays. Obviously I was disappointed, but I secretly thought it would be safer for my parents if I stayed here. We said our goodbyes and wished each other well, and then we hung up.

I had gotten up so much earlier than everyone that morning that I had decided to head to bed early. I slowly made my way up the stairs. I passed by the thin hallway with no doors and made my way to my room. I checked on Thorn and poured some more corn into her dish. Thorn was now hopping everywhere. Her leg had healed, but her wing was still injured. I slipped out of my clothes and into my cozy pajamas. I had Mr. Kunkle put an extra blanket on my bed so that I wouldn't be as cold. I pulled down the first sheet and crawled into my soft bed. That night I slept like a baby. I had no dreams and slept the entire night.

I awoke the next day from one of the best sleeps I had ever had. I was full of energy and very happy. I was singing to myself and dancing around in my big room enjoying life. I was enjoying life until I turned back towards my bed.

I dropped the hairbrush I was using as a microphone and my stomach dropped. My stomach dropped so low it was in the basement. But what wasn't in the basement were the little girls. At least they weren't last night. My bed sheets and pillows were all covered in tiny hand prints and foot prints. The handprints were on my bed in what seemed like baby powder, while the footprints were soot from the basement.

I leaped out into the hall and ran to Simon's room, knocking on Gilbert's door as I passed. The boys inspected my room as I went to go find Mr. Kunkle in his study.

Claire Hyatt

Mr. Kunkle had his glasses on his nose so I knew he was onto something. Sampson stood nearby. The three of us walked back to my room slowly. Sampson clinking as his walk carried a steady tune. Why he didn't just float instead of walking was beyond me.

Inside my room Mr. Kunkle got the same expression Gilbert and Simon had. We all knew it was the little girls, but nobody knew why. "Miss Aria, I'd say you're being haunted." Mr. Kunkle said. Sampson stared at the bed in awe. He exchanged a few words with Mr. Kunkle followed by many ahas and mhmms.

That day was very uneventful, besides the fact that I'm apparently being haunted by two dead little girls. That freaks me out a bit, especially because of what had happened in the basement. "I think it's cool that you're haunted." Gilbert reassured me, "besides Sampson is haunting Mr. Kunkle and he's not a bad guy. Sampson is helping us prepare for the dark force."

Dammit I was terrified. But maybe Gilbert was right. It couldn't be that bad. Real life is not like horror movies.

That night was a night that I wouldn't want to sleep alone, but I wasn't at home, and I was all by myself.

Claire Hyatt

Chapter Seven

The next few weeks went by very fast. Mr. Kunkle remained in his office studying random stuff, while Gilbert, Simon and I followed ghosts around the mansion trying to find out more. The little girls hadn't shown themselves to me yet, but their presence was everywhere. Faint giggles came in the background of everything I did. They followed me like lost puppies. Whenever I spoke too loud I was harshly shushed by the girls, and I was constantly being told to come find them. I didn't need to find them, they would always find me.

I was completely fine with the dead now, as long as I wasn't being possessed or physically touched.

Christmas was just a few days away and so far nobody talked about leaving for the holidays, at least not until the phone call. The phone never rang for anyone but me, so when the phone rang during breakfast I got up to answer it. The person on the other end of the line was not looking for me, this elderly sounding man asked for Mr. Kunkle.

I walked into the dining room and told him the phone was for him. His smile dropped and he rose to go retrieve the phone. I sat back down on my side of the table. Gilbert and Simon sat on the other side. The table sat 20, which actually isn't that big of a table, not compared to the house anyways.

We sat in silence and waited for Mr. Kunkle to return. A few minutes later when Mr. Kunkle returned, he was not smiling. It almost appeared as if he had been crying. Mr. Kunkle began to speak, "I'm sorry but I have to leave. I have to leave immediately, and I can't bring any of you. I hope to make it back for the holidays."

"Why ar--"

"My friend, another seer, living a few hours away has just been killed." His face dropped and he left the room. He didn't even give us any time to give our condolences.

I suppose Mr. Kunkle had called a cab because someone knocked the silver knockers saying he was here to pick up Mr. Kunkle. Mr. Kunkle got ready very quickly. He came down the stairs with a suitcase, he nodded to me, said goodbye and walked out the door.

Claire Hyatt

He left us all with no warning or anything. The house felt so empty without him in it. We had the house to ourselves; well not really, the abundance of ghosts never left us alone.

The next morning I woke up early and chilly. The giggles of girls in my room silenced Thorn. I went down into the kitchen to a cold pot of water. It was strange knowing I was the only one awake. I boiled some water, made tea and went to my comfy maroon chair in the library. The bright sunlight shone in through the window blinding my view for a second before disappearing behind a puffy white cloud. The snow that had piled itself up was now melting away into the ground that was thriving for water.

I took a very deep breath taking in the smell of old books. I looked around the library fascinated at how big and amazing it really was. I scanned the perfectly lined shelves full of differently coloured books. I looked at the ladder and noticed that a book was missing from the very top shelf. I scanned the room and noticed that on the other side of the library a book was open on a table.

Being the nice person I am, I thoughtfully went over to go return the book so the library would be clean for Mr. Kunkle when he came back. Although I'm thoughtful, I'm also quite nosy. I plopped down on the hard chair and picked up the book.

The book was covered in dust. What the hell, how long has this been here? I could hear the boys waking up upstairs. I blew the dust off the open pages in the book. I looked at the cover, *The Legends Of Old England*.

I flipped back to the page that was left open. It was on an old wives tale dealing with crows. That's strange, I thought. Gilbert drowsily stumbled into the library. "What're you looking at Aria?" Gilbert asked. He peered over my shoulder.

"Do you think your brother was looking at this? It's been open for a while, dust was accumulating."

"I'm not sure, let's ask him," Gilbert smiled at me, "SIMONNNN! COME HERE!" Gilbert shouted. His voice echoed through the entire library and stopped when Simon walked through the door. Gilbert asked if Simon was looking at the book.

"No, not that I recall," Simon replied, " hmm, Crows are a sign of death, and it's said that whenever a bird hits your window, someone close to you is going to die."

"Mr. Kunkle must've been prepared." I said. Now I was sounding crazy, "but that's just an old legend, it's not true." The boys nodded. I put the book back and the three of us went to get breakfast.

Chapter Eight

"It's hard to believe that Christmas is actually tomorrow." Gilbert stated during breakfast. I had almost forgotten about Christmas.

"Why aren't the two of you going home for Christmas?" I asked. Simon smiled at Gilbert and then to me. I felt very awkward in that moment, so I just filled my face with sausage.

"We don't really have any other home but here," Simon started, "our parents were killed when we were younger. But it's okay you didn't know that." It sure didn't feel okay to me, I felt like a total bitch. Of course there's no way I could've known that, but I didn't have to ask about their personal lives.

"Oh, I'm really sorry." I didn't have any idea what to say beyond that. I thought losing my grandparents was hard, but I can't even imagine how hard it was for the two of them to lose their parents when they were little. Every time I talked about my parents, I can only imagine how terrible it made them feel. I felt like a complete idiot. I chose to avoid talking about home for a while.

Trying to stop the awkward silence, I said, "So what are the three of us going to do for our awesome Christmas together." Simon and Gilbert both lit up and Gilbert began chuckling.

"You just unleashed a monster." Gilbert announced. Simon then began chattering about all of the food he was going to make. I was happy with that, we were all happy, until Simon told us that we were going to help him. We all laughed at the thought of Gilbert cooking, but what they didn't know was how bad I was at it too. I burned toast, remember.

"Christmas is very much about food, both sweet and savoury. Christmas turkey, baked glazed ham, sausages and smoked salmon sit side by side with rich, fruity Christmas cake, Christmas pudding and an excess of chocolates." Simon exclaimed. He was just pumped for life. "The fun part is that we get to go out and buy it ourselves."

I'd only left the mansion a few times since I'd arrived, but I had never gone into town. Helmsley is a market town and civil parish in the Ryedale district of North Yorkshire, England.

We walked for quite some time until we reached the outside of the town. It's a handsome old place full of old houses, historic coaching inns and a cobbled square, where every day is market day.

The sun was shining even brighter and the day was warming up. All the water that had steadied on the ground had already soaked deep into the earth. As the three of us walked by I began to notice the busyness of the place. I had thought that this town was home to just 3000 people.

As we walked further I realized half of these people, were dead. These ghosts were everywhere, and I couldn't even differentiate between the living and nonliving. I began to wonder how many people I had seen in Ohio who were part of the undead society of earth.

We quickly checked off all of the items on the list we made for tomorrow's Christmas dinner. We had visited roughly all of the stores in town, including some of the vegetable stands that remained open during the winter months, even though they had no vegetables just crafts. We filled six paper bags full of groceries for Christmas, including some extra chocolates for later.

When we walked home, I tried avoiding the faces of the dead. I didn't want one to follow me home. Although it would be better to have a bunch of ghosts in the mansion that looked like normal people, not all bloody and decaying.

We walked back through the gates and a brush of cold air passed by me. I decided we should take a detour around where the lady in red walks daily not to interrupt anything. Instead of running into the lady in red, we ran into Coraline. Gilbert tipped his hat and we shared hellos. We walked into the house and Simon insisted on putting away the groceries himself. He was very controlling when it came to food. Gilbert and I decided to go and hang out in the library while Simon put away our food and made supper. That night's supper was quite boring, and would never compare to our Christmas supper.

Christmas wasn't very eventful and Mr. Kunkle came home around noon. He arrived when we were preparing dinner. Even though we hadn't received any presents our supper made up for it. We had decorated the dining hall with streamers, candles and cute holiday decorations. The food was beyond phenomenal. I had so many servings of mashed potatoes I could've exploded.

That night I was sleeping like a baby, however, somebody during the night was moving around. I was startled awake by a sudden noise only to catch a glimpse of a dark figure standing by my bed.

The ka-clinking in the hallway scared the dark figure away. I slipped out of my bed and walked towards the door. The ka-clinking continued. I began to think about the noise. It sounded very familiar then I realized it was Sampson. Why would he be walking around so late at night? Sampson was only ever around when Mr. Kunkle was with him. I slowly reached for the door handle. But then I was stopped by a sudden hand on my shoulder.

I swung around to see the figure again. This time, I could see the figure's face and clothes. It was an attractive young male dressed in a khaki military uniform. I opened my mouth to speak when a brush of wind blew past taking the ghost with it. I turned back around to face the door and there was a damn bloody child handprint dripping down the door frame.

I worked up the courage to open the door. The door slowly creaked open, only for me to find bloody footprints leading down the hallway. I debated walking a few steps just to knock on Gilbert's door, but my curiosity once again got the best of me and I headed in the directions of the footprints. They lead down the hallway to the side of the house where no one goes. I was quite hesitant after the appearance of the falling apart boy but I continued walking.

The air was cold very cold and goose bumps covered my skin. Then suddenly something pushed at my back and I fell forward. I hit my head on something as I fell. I tried to stand back up, but something was pressing me down. I began to lose breath, my throat tightened. Someone was cutting off my air supply. I felt hands around my neck. I was crawling along the floor as I slowly ran out of air. My lungs screamed for air. I crawled down a new hallway that I hadn't noticed before. I couldn't go any further. I had reached a dead end.

I almost gave up, and accepted my death, and then my mother's words rang in my ears "Glory isn't never falling, but getting back up when you do." I had no idea if that related to my situation, but I was definitely getting back up. I used the last breath I had to stand up. Air was returned to my burning lungs.

My eyes had adjusted to the dark hallway and I observed my surroundings. I must have ventured further into the north end of the house than I thought. This was a very unexplored mansion from my knowledge. The wallpaper had changed from pale striped to flowers. I can see how it would have been beautiful wallpaper at one point, but mold and mildew had eaten away at it stealing the rich colour it once had.

I looked at the wall that I had hit with my head before I almost died. It was a door. I tried the cool metal handle on the door, but it was bolted shut. Disappointed I kicked the door with rage.

The rotting door didn't budge. I had hoped for it to fall down, but I was mistaken. I trudged my way back down the hallways that turned and turned until I found the grand staircase. A feeling of relief washed over me as I saw Simon walking downstairs with a cup of tea.

I rushed down the stairs after him. Talking a mile a minute I explained to him what had happened to me. He placed his tea down and ran outside while I grabbed Gilbert who was still sleeping.

I dragged a groggy Gilbert down the hall until we met up with Simon at the hallway which brings you to the north side of the house. Simon as much as he didn't want to go to the north end, he followed me.

I slowly led them to the door trying to remember where I had come from. Trying to avoid awkward silence between the half-asleep kid, and the fear-torn one I decided to ask why Simon hated the North side. Gilbert looked at me with remorse for his brother. Simon's answer was unexpected.

"Betty-Anne, she was my best friend. A seer just like us. She used to live here before everyone left. She loved adventure just as much as us, but more importantly, she loved to paint. She could paint out our stories so well that it was if you were actually on the adventure with us," his throat caught his words. "One day she disappeared to her bedroom on this side of the house. She didn't say much all morning. I should've asked if she was okay. But I didn't. She was found on the ground below her balcony the next morning. I don't know what happened. I should've done more..."

Tears swelled in Simon's eyes and he couldn't continue. I decided not to push him and I let the topic drop as we approached the door that was bolted shut. Simon lifted up those big rusty pliers with strength I didn't think he had. He tore the locks right off the door.

The door swung right open. "You shouldn't have brought THEM," a little girl's voice said. "We told you we didn't want them," another girl's voice said. It was the girls from the basement; the ones who were haunting me.

I looked at Gilbert and Simon and stepped forward alone. This room was a child's room. There was a little wooden rocking horse whose paint had been chipped away by the years. There were two child-sized canopy beds side by side full of dust. Dust had claimed most of the room including the wooden dolls. There were pale peach walls that had tiny clowns on them and in the corner of the room was a chest. A chest made of cedar that was padlocked.

We took a step forward into the room. Faint giggling was heard from somewhere in the room. I looked to Gilbert and Simon with fear. Our mouths dropped open. Gilbert then began to point towards the bed. I turned and noticed a small stripped wooden ball roll out from underneath the bed and hit the chest.

The chest called to me. I walked towards it as Gilbert and Simon entered the room. "Please." The girls' voices begged in unison. "Help us"

Simon handed me the pliers and I broke off the lock. Only then did I see the blood covering the chest. I was frozen in place. I did not want to see what was inside that chest.

"Aria, please help us before HE does."

"Who is HE? The man from the basement? What does HE want?"

"HE wants to help us move on, but you can help us too. HE is coming back again and this time HE is stronger." The two girls appeared side by side in the doorway behind us.

One of the girls was two years younger than the other, but they were both dressed in matching baby blue dresses covered in dirt. Their eyes held fear, yet they also showed hope. They both had hope in me. I turned and opened the chest.

All five of us bent over to peer inside the chest. Two tiny skeletons were stuffed inside the chest wearing baby blue dresses. "Thank you Aria, you have freed us," the girls softly spoke with much gratefulness. And they both slowly disappeared.

We all looked to each other in disbelief before silently leaving the room.

Claire Hyatt

Chapter Nine

Mr. Kunkle's only explanation for the girls in the chest was "this is a big house that holds many secrets." I could tell that Mr. Kunkle maybe knew more than he telling me.

The day dragged on slowly with mixed emotions and confusion. I sat in the library with Thorn as she hopped around on the floor. I sat and stared out the window with sorrow. "Don't beat yourself up over it Aria, you helped them and that's all you can do," Gilbert came up behind me and sat down, "there's never an explanation as to why someone would do something so terrible."

I offered up a smile before Simon came in with three cups of tea. We sat together for the rest of the afternoon reading and talking and enjoying the life we were appreciative to have.

The next morning I was awoken once again by the cold. I half expected to see the mysterious army man from the previous night, but all it was, was an open window.

Since it was Sunday I got to call my parents. Our chat was cut short when Mr. Kunkle insisted that Sampson had gotten him a step closer to finding out what was coming for us. I reluctantly hung up the phone. Mr. Kunkle got two rings into his phone call until he realized that the friend he was calling is dead. He mumbled something under his breath then slipped away to his office.

I decided not to call my parents back; instead I thought I'd go talk to Coraline. She was where she usually is, hidden away in the row of beautiful trees. The trees were even more miraculous with frost covering the branches. I tightened my red scarf as I approached Coraline.

First thing I thought of as she slowly floated towards me with a warm smile was the little girls' smiles as they faded to the afterlife. Then a question popped out of my mouth. "Did they ever find your body?"

Coraline looked a little shocked but she answered with a smile, "Why yes they did, not too long after I was dead." I gave her a quizzical look, and she continued, "I suppose you're probably wondering why those little girls 'passed on' after their bodies have been found, and I haven't, even though I've been found?"

"They didn't have anything to stay back for, they already had each other. However, for me, I'm still waiting for someone," she smiled even bigger.

I smiled back and let the topic drop, and Gilbert brought me out some hot cocoa to warm my chilled hands. I stayed out in the cold talking to her until dark.

That night in my sleep I dreamt of a young woman, but I was in the woman's body. I heard her talking, I cried her tears, and I felt her pain. In the dream I walked inside the door and wiped my muddy brown slippers on the welcome mat. I placed them in a cubby. I walked into a bedroom when I placed my lantern next to a picture on the dresser. The picture was of a young man and girl on their wedding day. They looked very happy together. Then I stared into the mirror at a foreign face. Tears streamed down her rosy cheeks. I wiped away the mascara running down. I took out the bun she wore upon her head and ran my fingers through the brown hair, blew out the lantern and left the bedroom.

I walked back towards the door almost thinking I was walking out the door again but I was not in control of this body. I bent down and pulled the welcome mat back. A trap door lay there. I opened the door and went inside. I was in a cellar. There was a musty smell and canned jars of pickled carrots. There was a pillow on the ground next to some straw. I sat next to the pillow. I leaned my head next to the wall when I heard a thump on the cellar door. My mood immediately rose. "Could it be my love?" I exclaimed to myself. I reached up to push the cellar door open. I was locked in. "Hello!" I shouted. No answer. I must have been hearing things.

I pushed even harder on the cellar door and it wouldn't budge. Panic fell over my body. I reached up to the cellar door screaming and scratching at the wood. I looked to the unfamiliar hands when I felt searing pain. My fingers were bloody and I had splinters all over my hands. My nails continued to scratch at the wood leaving claw marks in place of the wood.

I scratched and scratched until my fingernails were filed down to nothing but blood and skin. I gave it all I could. I suddenly began to get quite tired. I lay down on the cold ground. "He hasn't come home; all I was trying to do was be in a better spot to hear his footsteps walking through my door, now I am trapped." I breathed out using the last of my energy. I fell asleep in a puddle of my own salty tears.

In my sleep I grew very cold. I was aware of how cold I was, as if I was paralyzed, I could not move. I could not wake. My blood grew cold. I felt my heart beats slow. I could not wake up. I tried to scream but nothing came out. I could not wake up. I was dying. I felt my heart stop in the cold. I was Coraline.

Chapter Ten

I woke from the dream in a panicked cold sweat. The sun was rising so it had to be later than 8am. I sat up in bed and watched as a tall figure disappeared out of the corner. I shrugged it off and went for breakfast. Tea and biscuits warmed my body.

After breakfast I decided to go to Mr. Kunkle's study for a visit. "Ah hello Miss Reed, what brings you to the darkness of my study on such a nice winter day?"

Mr. Kunkle's study was very roomy. A dark wooden desk was in the center, taking up the majority of the room. The desk was covered in countless papers in many languages. Only one painting hung on the wall; it was a tiny blue sailboat on a big open sea all alone. He sat in a comfortable black cushion chair. And two leather arm chairs faced away from me in front of the desk. The walls were engraved with swirls that held many emotions as they circled around the room.

"I just stopped to have a chat." I said quietly. It felt wrong to speak loudly in such a soothing environment.

Claire Hyatt

"Is something bothering you missy?" Mr. Kunkle asked peacefully, "I know it can be hard to see what you saw the other day in that chest."

"I will be okay, I've just been wondering lately, about what it is that is coming for us," I spat out.

"I don't think HE is onto our trail yet, whoever HE is, but that doesn't mean we have much time." He adjusted his glasses, "The greatest gift you have been given is the gift of your imagination. Everything that now exists was once imagined, and that's all I've come to know these past few months."

Searching the carvings on the walls for an answer, I stared past him in wonderment. "So you're saying it's just made up, and that nothing is coming for us? We have nothing to worry about." A rush of relief passed over me.

"No, not quite dear," Mr. Kunkle's voice went flat, "whatever it is that's coming for us could be anything. It could be anything in your wildest dream. It's just we have no idea what's coming. We could be so off."

My stomach dropped and I lost my train of thought. I had nothing to say. I was scared. "How can we stop something that is unknown but so dangerous that it has already taken the lives of many people?" and that's when Gilbert and Simon walked in. The room went silent.

Simon had suggested we just pack up and leave, keep whatever was coming for us away, but Mr. Kunkle solemnly declined. "You cannot run away from your fears; you must sometime fight it out or perish, and if that be so, why not now."

The room had once again silenced until Sampson made an appearance. Mr. Kunkle ushered us away as he had business to tend to.

Since I wasn't feeling up for the mood of research or ghost hunting I decided to go take a nap. My nap was a failure because when I walked into my room that dark shadow lurked in my corner and I was forced to go on a ghost hunt.

Instead of this man disappearing like usual, he stepped out into the sunlight. A smirk appeared on his face. His dog tag glistened in the sunshine and I studied his body. Past his green long sleeve shirt I noticed he was holding something. I refused to let him go away so I began to speak, "I know who you are."

Claire Hyatt

He held his hand up and showed me the picture in his hand; it was a picture of Coraline. "Follow me," I exclaimed.

Chapter Eleven

I led him out the back door of the mansion quietly and brought him to the beginning of the trees. I was so overjoyed to be the one to reunite the two torn apart lovers. I couldn't wait to see the looks in both their eyes. We walked down the long row of trees as a small amount of snow fell from the sky. It had been a few days since the last snowfall. The snow was fluffy and white and it stuck to the branches of the trees like a winter wonderland.

The army man walked slowly to the bench beyond the trees. He left no footprints behind. I heard a squeak of a door and peered over my shoulder to see Gilbert and Simon standing in the doorway. They gave me thumbs up and I beamed.

We stopped at the antique cement bench and he took in a deep breath anticipating what was to come. We stood for a good while before the man looked at me and took a step away from the bench with sorrow. I took a step back as well, and that's when Coraline showed up.

The emotion between the two when they saw each other was so strong I could feel it in the thumps of my heart beating. There was a lump in my throat and tears swelled in my eyes. When they embraced a spark lit up the surroundings. The trees never looked brighter. Their ages decreased back to the day they wed.

Even though it was the winter months, a sweet aroma of blossoms filled the air and little pink buds grew on the bushes nearby which then turned into bright pink flowers. A light shone from the heavens down on the two and they radiated with purple glow.

They both shared a look of love. The two happily looked towards me with a head nod. I knew in that moment how truly grateful Coraline was to be reunited.

This was her time and she was ready to leave earth. The light from the heavens shone so brightly that all I could see was white. A feeling of pure satisfaction and joy passed over me and I knew that they had passed on.

The joy and love was short lived when I saw Gilbert rushing towards me screaming. He grabbed my arm and dragged me into the house. We made it inside just before the earthquake hit. The sky had turned a dark grey and there was no sign outside that something wonderful had just happened moments before. I shook in Gilbert's arms terrified of what had just taken place. I watched out the library window as strong winds blew apart the beautiful row of trees that Coraline had once treasured.

"I think it is," Gilbert said addressing the elephant in the room, "It is HE." Simon and I looked at Gilbert with amazement. He had read our minds. Whatever it was that *was* coming for us and was *far away,* HE was now here.

Immediately we went to Mr. Kunkle's office and interrupted his and Sampson's deep conversation. He stood silent for a while and shook his head. "I told you we could be off, and we certainly are more off than we thought," Mr. Kunkle admitted. Everyone knew they couldn't avoid this thing forever. "We are putting the house in lockdown."

Lockdown meant we had to be careful with everything and limit going outside for silly things. To achieve this we needed enough food to supply us for at least a month. Simon had gone shopping for groceries not a week earlier. When Simon shops, he really shops, so we would have food for quite some time. The only thing running low in the house at the time was pickles. And between the four of us, we went through a lot of pickles, trust me.

None of us could last the week or month or however long we were in lockdown without our pickles, so we went to get some from the root cellar. Mr. Kunkle remained with Sampson in the mansion while Gilbert, Simon and I went to the root cellar.

Chapter Twelve

The root cellar wasn't in the house or basement, it was beside Sampson's little shed in the ground. Gilbert put the key that Mr. Kunkle gave him in the rusty padlock. The lock needed a little encouraging as the key wasn't working and so I grabbed an axe from Sampson's shed. The axe was just the right encouragement the lock needed, one hit and it opened.

I brushed the snow off the handles and yanked the two doors open. Cool musty air flew out towards us and I gagged at the putrid smell. I wasn't sure if something had died in there or if the accumulation of vinegar and garlic had taken a toll on the place.

The cellar was even colder in winter months. I could see my breath and I blew out in big breaths thinking to myself how I used to pretend I was a dragon when winter came in Ohio when I was younger. I could see out of the corner of my eye that Simon and Gilbert were also studying their breaths. Even if there was light down there you would not be able to see past the many rows of shelves that were occupied by pickled vegetables and various jellies and jams. The silence was broken when something dropped somewhere in the dark cellar.

"Alright so let's grab as many jars as we can and get the hell out of this cellar." Gilbert said.

"Good plan," I said. I think Gilbert vaguely winked at me before turning and scavenging the shelves. Simon had already started and was carrying three jars of pickled carrots.

We filled the backpack up with various jars, unsure just what each jar held. I tried to reach to the very top of the shelf for a strange orange jar, and when Simon and Gilbert could not reach it either we opted out. Walking away from the shelf, a jar flew and hit Simon in the back of the head. It was that damn orange jar. We swung around to see a very old wrinkly lady. Gilbert appeared as if he was going to run away but my hand on his shoulder made him stay.

This lady didn't seem very scary, she reminded me of a grandma. Her wrinkles defined her as old, and her droopy eye made it seem as if she had died of a stroke. "Sorry," the old lady croaked out with her raspy voice.

She was not here to hurt us, only help us, or so I thought.

All was well in the cellar and we wasted as little time as possible. It wasn't until we were climbing up the rotting ladder leading out of the cellar that something happened. Gilbert had said ladies first, and so I got out of the cellar first with Gilbert close behind. Simon had claimed he was the manliest and could go last. Once Gilbert was out of the dark cellar, we both peered in looking for Simon. The doors flew up and slammed down, locking Simon in the cellar.

A maniacal cackling from the cellar surfaced, followed by a scared boy's scream.

Gilbert and I tore at the doors trying to open them but it was as if they were bolted shut. Simon's scream continued. Gilbert was livid, "Stop this nonsense!" He hollered. He reached for the rusty old axe and started hacking at the door. His adrenaline was pumping and nothing could stop him.

The broken doors flew open and out sailed Simon. He landed on his ass and stained the snow with blood. He had landed on his glasses, breaking them. Tears streamed down his face. Simon looked so helpless in that moment; his brother looked down at him in sorrow.

Mr. Kunkle walked out and saw Simon lying in the snow. He ran back inside and called the ambulance. Simon was immediately rushed to the hospital and treated for his cuts and bruises. The doctor explained how it looked as if Simon was attacked by a rabid dog. His cuts were already infected and if he wasn't brought in, the probability of him dying was 50:50.

"This was no dog," Simon peeped out. Mr. Kunkle shook his head and told Simon to save it for later.

Simon was told to stay the night at the hospital. Mr. Kunkle returned home, while Gilbert and I spent the night in the most uncomfortable arm chairs ever. So much for staying in lockdown.

In the morning Simon returned home. He was still weak from the traumatic events from the previous day but that would heal with time. Luckily nothing had been broken and with a few stitches in a few weeks you wouldn't even notice any injury. The doctor hadn't fully discovered what had happened to Simon but he helped him regardless and asked little questions. The doctor remained silent but we wouldn't.

As soon as we helped Simon into his room to rest on the bed Gilbert, Mr. Kunkle and I hounded him with questions. Simon wasn't much help though, the cellar was dark, and all he could tell us was that it definitely had human hands and was unlike anything he had ever experienced from a spirit.

Mr. Kunkle nodded in recognition of Simon as he got up to leave the room. He had his hand on the door knob about to turn the knob when he turned back to us. "These entities are negatively affecting us and are more powerful now than ever. The spirits are the problem, not the outside world. I feel it is best to stay away from all spirits from now on."

Claire Hyatt

Chapter Thirteen

Days passed and Simon's health was already greatly improving. No spirits had chosen to bother us after the decision to ignore them. All was going well until a small wooden train decided to make its way slowly into Simon's room where Simon, Gilbert and I were all sitting.

I sat in the red felt chair and looked across the room at Simon who sat upright in his bed. His bed didn't look very comfortable; it was rock hard and looked like the mattress was made of mahogany wood just like the rest of the bed. Gilbert sat perched on the foot stool just in front of the window. My gaze shifted to his with worry when a young boy followed the train. He was the same boy I saw in the north end.

The boy's face, however didn't fall apart like last time, instead he decided to scale the wall. He sat upon the door frame watching us until he swooped across the wall and landed in front of the opened closet door. He began waving wildly as if trying to get our attention. We paid him no attention, avoiding the boy's stare.

He eventually gave up and slipped out of the room followed by the small wooden train, whose squeaky wheel almost drove me crazy. The boy and the squeaky train had disappeared once in the hallway and the three of us sat in silence for quite some time before Gilbert offered to go make us some tea. Twenty some minutes later Gilbert returned, with no tea.

"I just saw Mr. Kunkle," Gilbert puffed out, "he was sneaking around with Sampson."

"I thought we all agreed to no spirits for a while!" I exclaimed, "That's not fair. We also have spirits around the grounds that we're close with, but we're choosing to ignore them." Then I thought it through how Sampson had been helping us this whole time and was no danger to any of us. "Actually we should just let them be, I don't know how long Mr. Kunkle has known Sampson, but he trusts him and I guess we should too."

Later that same night when I was sleeping my bed began to shake, it felt like another earthquake like the day Coraline moved on. I just held the sheets up to my face and ignored it as much as I could.

"Could this potentially mean that HE is still getting closer?" I asked Mr. Kunkle at breakfast. Yes and no was his only response before returning to his black pudding and baked beans. This obviously meant he had no damn clue about a thing anymore. And I was just to accept it, because that's how it is and nothing was changing.

That afternoon it did nothing but pour. The snow was melting rapidly as springtime approached. I sat in the library with Thorn nearly all day watching the rain drops fall down the window. Thorn must have been watching too because she decided it was a brilliant idea to test out her fully healed wings by jumping up trying to see out the window. She flapped her wings as hard as she could but wasn't getting much air.

The smart bird that she is, she hopped onto me and balanced on my head. Flapping her wings, her gaze set on the window sill, she jumped. Instead of falling with a thud like usual, she began flying. She landed gracefully on the sill. Adrenaline was still pumping in her veins; I could see it in her posture and eyes.

I called Gilbert and Simon to come from the kitchen as quickly as possible. They arrived when Thorn was making her way through the library, up and down rows of shelves. Her confidence never faltered.

We began clapping and laughing, which is when Mr. Kunkle came in. "I just came to see what the commotion was, ah Miss Thorn has finished being pampered I see." I could sense Sampson standing behind the door, and almost acknowledged him out of habit.

It was Simon who piped up. "Sampson can come in sir," he politely said to Mr. Kunkle, "we understand. You don't have to hide him from us," Mr. Kunkle nodded graciously and Sampson ka-clinked his way into the room.

We were all enjoying ourselves until Thorn disappeared behind a book shelf. We all walked in that direction when we heard a thud on the other side of the library. Thorn had hit the window.

"You stupid bird!" Gilbert rang out as he ran to go pick Thorn up. This time, there would be no fun bird sanctuary to build, because Thorn was indeed dead. We didn't wait for the rain to stop. We bowed our head in the rain saying our last goodbye as we buried Thorn in the rose bushes beneath the library window, the same window she had ran into twice.

I only shed a few tears when I was alone in the shower, so no one could see that I was upset over the loss of my friend. Days flew by quickly filled with rain and more rain. The only thing I felt like doing was eating; there was nothing else to do.

One thought crossed my mind in between two of my ten meals a day. *Crows are a sign of death, and it's said that whenever a bird hits your window, someone close to you is going to die.* I never spoke these thoughts to anyone, because I didn't feel the need to. Everyone was thinking the same thing.

At dinner Mr. Kunkle tried to bring it up, claiming within his laughter that we are just three superstitious youngins. But we all knew he felt the same way. He was aware that it had happened once and it would indeed happen again.

Stupid little things continued happening; people would get scratched in the night, bite marks were found on our ankles, earthquakes continued. But it wasn't until spring rolled around, as soon as the last pile of snow disappeared that things really started getting bad.

Sampson was with Mr. Kunkle almost 24/7, leaving us no time for any questions or comfort. All of us were still worried about people we were close with. I called my parents almost every night just to check in on them. They continued to ask me "Are you sure everything is alright Aria? You seem to be calling an awful lot lately." My answer was always the same, "I just miss you and love you both lots, that's all."

Claire Hyatt

Chapter Fourteen

I was brushing my teeth after I had gotten out of the shower. The water tasted like dirt from all the mineral content coming from the well. I was in my purple robe with a white towel twisted up in my hair upon the top of my head.

I spit my last fluoride mouthful of my toothpaste into the sink and looked up into the mirror. The mirror had rust stains on the edges much like the rest of the cast iron and porcelain in the bathroom. I thought I saw a spider web in the corner of the mirror and reached over for a cloth to wipe it with.

The cloth did nothing because it turned out it wasn't a spider web. It was a crack that I hadn't noticed before. I touched the fold of the crack with my finger nail and the crack grew. Embarrassed to break the mirror I took my finger off and continued getting ready. After washing my face I had noticed the crack spread across the entire top of the mirror. I knew I hadn't done that. Taking my hair out and brushing it with the metal brush I stared into my reflection.

I didn't have the skinniest face, my cheeks puffed out a bit and freckles covered my nose. It appeared as if I always had tired eyes. A sunburn always took a place under them. My hair, thin and a healthy brown colour stood out. My hair was always very smooth and shiny. My bangs never worked how I wanted so I just tucked it behind my ear to dry.

I didn't mind my face; I actually felt pretty all the time no matter how I looked. I was pretty. My face had no blemishes at all, and it stayed soft. And then, the mirror smashed in it.

I screamed and dropped to the floor holding my face. I lay there bleeding heavily. Blood seeped into the creases of the square tiles on the floor. I watched as the blood poured into those creases taking different paths like an over flowing stream. I sat up to yell again, realizing how much I was hurting and how lucky I was that the glass had missed my eyes.

Once I had let out a scream for help and heard footsteps running down the hall I swallowed and beheld my blood that had seeped into the floor tiles.

Claire Hyatt

I hadn't even realized I was screaming until Gilbert grabbed me by the shoulders to steady me, and then he picked me up. I looked into his eyes and I saw fear as he saw my injuries. His fear turned into horror when he saw my blood on the floor that spelt out *run*.

And that is just what we did. Run. Well I didn't run I was thrown over Gilbert's shoulder as he ran down the hall, down the stairs and right out the door. The entire time he was shouting out orders. I began getting tired. My vision blurred and I felt fuzzy. The last thing I heard was "Aria please, stay with me"

I woke in the hospital. The doctor was probably wondering what was going on in our house. I writhed in pain. I pursed my lips as I opened my eyes. The only time I remember feeling any pain close to this was two summers ago when I fell down the stairs and broke my arm. I could feel my heart beating in my brain.

I reached up to touch my face in hopes of relieving some pain and a hand grabbed my wrist. "Don't touch, doctor's orders," Simon smiled, "She's awake!"

Gilbert, Mr. Kunkle, two nurses and Sampson came storming in. Sampson of course could not be seen by anyone but us seers.

In my peripheral vision I could see something black on my face. I turned towards the mirror and saw that my face was covered, and I mean covered, in stitches.

The first thought in my head was 'how am I going to explain this to my parents' and then I remembered that they were an ocean away and they never had to find out. The second thought in my mind was how scary that experience was. I did not want to return to the mansion. But I didn't want to stay anywhere else either. I was safe nowhere.

Whatever was coming could find anyone anywhere. My thoughts were proven when the door slammed shut making me shiver. "It must be the wind." One of the nurses stated. But what they couldn't see was the ghost in a blood soaked white gown that had entered the room. I was getting really tired of this. She didn't say or do anything before disappearing not to return.

I was allowed to go home that same day; the doctor said he wouldn't have to have me back to check on my cuts because the stitches were dissolvable. Luckily my cuts weren't too deep.

I was scared to sleep that night. I felt vulnerable even though my body and brain had no damage, only my face. I was surprised Mr. Kunkle isn't worrying more. Does he know something I don't, because I'm pretty worried about the safety of myself and everyone else? I managed to fall asleep in only three hours. It was midnight when I woke up. Well I was woken up. Just great.

I could feel compression on the bed like someone was sitting on the end of it. I decided I didn't want to know, so I just ignored it. Then the compression became more like when your cat is crawling from the bottom of the bed up to your head to sleep beside you. I opened one eye to confirm my contemplations. There was no one there.

I stopped caring when it happened all the time when I had first moved here, but now, it seemed different. It was like I was experiencing it for the first time all over again, and I was scared. I didn't like to admit that I was scared, but I was and time was up.

I quickly got up out of bed and walked across the hall to Gilbert's room. I was more comfortable there. I didn't even wake him; I just plopped down on the sofa across from his bed and fell into a blissful sleep.

The week went by very fast but it was very painful. My face injuries were healing, which meant a lot of itching. If I didn't have stitches I would have been taking every chance I got to pick the scabs off.

The atmosphere in the house had begun to change and it began to feel crowded. The air seemed thicker and there was more whispering carried by the wind.

It felt as if when you were alone, you never really were alone.

I continued sleeping on Gilbert's sofa, afraid of the unknown. He would leave a pillow and blanket folded on the sofa for me. He wouldn't admit it, but I knew that he too was scared and appreciated me staying with him.

I realized I didn't need to sneak into his room when Mr. Kunkle made all of us stay in the same room one night. Mr. Kunkle then told us we should probably all sleep in the same room until things lighten up. "Safety in numbers," he told us.

He must have felt the presence of more entities around the house much like I did.

When Sunday rolled around I couldn't ignore the fact that I needed to call my parents. Not to tell them about my face, but to check if they were still okay. The chat was very brief because I reached my Mom right before she was heading out the door for work, and my Dad was already at work.

My Mom could sense some worry in my voice like always, and so she told me a nice walk would do the trick. I remembered how when springtime came in Ohio I would always go running, splashing through the puddles.

I slipped on my running shoes and headed out the door. It had finally stopped raining but little puddles made their home around the entire property.

I began running; I ran by Coraline's white cement bench and smiled. I continued running and ran out the gate towards town. The air was chilled and every inhale burned in my chest. I was very out of shape.

The town was empty as usual and dampness clung to the air. I ran through Helmsley in a big loop back towards the house. I wiped the sweat off my brows and began walking. I was chilled and a light long sleeve would have done the trick, but instead I wore a thin t-shirt. Just before I left town limits for home I decided to stop at one of the many coffee shops.

Concord Café was a dim lit comforting café. It was filled with many small tables with red sofa-like arm chairs to sit in.

The walls were brick and paintings covered them displaying many people in the town. It was like a wall of heroes. If you do anything to benefit the town you get on the wall. I noticed many old faces on the walls and very seldom young ones.

I walked towards the little old lady working the shop and asked for two green teas, one hazelnut vanilla coffee and a chocolate glazed croissant. The lady smiled through her wrinkles and turned to go make them.

She came back holding a tray with three hot drink take-out mugs on it. "I hope Eugene enjoys the croissant," she said. I gave a questioning look, then thanked the woman, handed her five pounds and made my way back to the house.

I walked slowly remembering where the row of trees used to be and felt the wind tangle my hair. It was so peaceful to be outside after a rainstorm. I gazed at the house in awe. It really was a big beautiful house. There were at least thirty windows on the east side of the house and one caught my attention. There was someone standing in it, dressed in all black. My bedroom. I hurried my pace and walked into the house.

Upon placing the tray in the kitchen I noticed Simon, Gilbert and Mr. Kunkle all seated at the dining table. My heart ached to go see who was standing in my room, but my better judgment told me just to take a seat.

"I brought you guys some tea from downtown," I said passing the tray to Gilbert and Simon, "and I didn't forget about you Mr. Kunkle, here's a croissant."

Gilbert and Simon's tea was most likely cold because my coffee certainly was and Mr. Kunkle's croissant was all squished and flaky. Nobody said a thing though; they all smiled and laughed about pointless things. For once in a few months, things seemed almost normal. That was until the screaming began.

We just could not cut a break. We all started to stand up, and Mr. Kunkle rose and motioned his hand for us to sit back down. He left the dining room.

All we could hear was a mix of screaming and laughing, it sounded like someone was enjoying being tortured. I covered my ears. Mr. Kunkle came back and with a chuckle he said "We are going crazy, the tea pot was screaming to let me know my tea was ready, ha-ha, and here I am thinking someone is in the other room being murdered."

I forced out a laugh, as did Simon and Gilbert. It was quite funny actually but something in the room just felt edgy. Then from down the hall I heard ka-clunk, ka-clunk, ka-clunk and knew that this was our signal to leave the room. Mr. Kunkle was very busy. As I walked up the stairs I heard Mr. Kunkle tell Sampson about the screaming tea pot and I faintly heard Sampson laugh. I smiled. That was the first time I have heard him laugh. He was happy even after death and he still had friends. It was adorable.

That night was the night that I lost it. I was sleeping on a mattress beside Simon's single bed. Gilbert slept on the long brown sofa just to the left of me beside the wall. The door was on the other side of the room, but I still heard it open. It was probably about 3am when it woke me up.

I watched as a hunchbacked figure made its way across the room. It just glided from the door way towards the sofa. In my haziness from just being awoken I thought it was Simon returning from the bathroom. Upon seeing that he was holding something I sat up and groggily asked, "Simon, what are you doing?" I looked to my right and saw Simon sleeping peacefully. And I looked to my left, there was Gilbert sleeping like a baby.

Shivers ran down my back. The figure had stopped moving but it was still facing more towards the wall. It's head cocked to the side and faced me. Not any part of it's body moved besides it's head. Then it shot across the room to me at like 100km/h. I screamed and Gilbert and Simon jumped awake. They saw the figure standing over me holding a hammer. Simon screamed and the figure disappeared.

Gilbert held me while Simon ran across the hall for Mr. Kunkle. Whatever that figure was it was going for Gilbert before I intervened.

It's face. It's terrible face was all I could see in my mind. It was damn scary and I never wanted to see it again.

Mr. Kunkle came in with so much worry spread on his face. I hadn't been injured this time but somehow it felt worse. Maybe it was because it was potentially going for someone else while they slept unknowingly. Would I have awoken the next day and Gilbert would be dead on the sofa if I didn't wake up? I would never know, and I didn't want to know. I was so done.

"I want to go home."

Claire Hyatt

Chapter Fifteen

"Now Aria, why don't you think this through before you do anything," Mr. Kunkle said in the morning, "Sampson advised me that it might not be the safest for you or your parents should you leave at this time."

He did have a point although he couldn't force me to stay. I felt as if my parents needed to know, I wasn't safe. Perhaps Mr. Kunkle was correct and that it would endanger my parents if I left or even if I had just told them. "But it isn't safe here and --" Mr. Kunkle cut me off.

"I know, and Aria I thought for a while you should go home but I was misguided." He cleared his throat, "Sampson said that I should not allow you to go home. And I trust in his instinct and with that being said, you are not to return home Aria Reed."

The way he had said my full name was in such a way that I sensed he was not himself, I felt as if I was being scolded by a mean principal after I had written something foul on the bathroom stall.

I knew he couldn't control me and maybe my best interests weren't in mind, however I couldn't just abandon the people I began caring about in Helmsley when they were in a tough situation. Especially not to go put my parents in danger back in Ohio.

Just then, at the breakfast table a fork began sliding towards me. It slid all on its own and stopped at the end of the table right in front of me. As soon as the fork stopped a piece of sausage flew off my plate and onto the floor. Once again my reasons to go home were revisited.

I was scared and it was my fear that wanted me to go home. However, I was also just a curious person and I wanted to figure everything out. I'm not going to lie, the spirit world was still a mystery to me and I wanted to learn more.

"Alright, you've given me no choice," I smirked, turning to Gilbert and Simon, who sat beside Mr. Kunkle, "I'll stay."

I knew I had done the right thing choosing to stay and help them, nonetheless I didn't feel good about my decision. My head had told me it was best to go home and I was following my head, but then my gut piped up and told me I was wanted here and I should just stay put. I always followed my gut. I was needed here and I would do what I was meant to do all along – whatever it was that I was meant to do. I silently hoped that I wasn't meant to die, not this young. I was just sixteen.

My destiny had brought me to this place and I would follow it through. Everything happens for a reason, right?

"If I'm staying we need to establish a way to stay safe in the night." I spoke up. Simon nodded in agreement whilst Gilbert spoke, "I think it'd be wise if we all take shifts in the night." I had thought Gilbert had a good idea. We would be getting a third less amount of sleep than that of which we usually would get, but it'd all be worth it. Besides, I haven't gotten much sleep lately anyways.

That night Simon took the first shift. Gilbert slept in Simon's bed while I drifted to sleep on the floor watching Simon on the sofa keeping watch. It felt as if I had just fallen asleep when Simon woke me saying, "Aria, it's your turn to take shift." I smiled and reluctantly got up off the floor and sat upon the sofa. Simon seated himself on the floor and snuggled up with the thin layer of blankets.

I was to stay watch for two and a half hours. My eye lids became heavy after ten minutes of staying watch. I wanted so desperately to just close my eyes for a few seconds. But knowing that if I did I would pass out in a blissful sleep, I forced my eyes to stay open. My head nodded back and forth effortlessly as I tried to stay attentive.

Two and a half hours passed by slowly but I didn't wait a second when my time was up to go tell Gilbert it was his turn. Gilbert rolled out of Simon's bed when I woke him. I settled into Simon's bed and passed out immediately. I was out cold until I smelt something burning beneath the strong smell of freshly ground coffee.

I jolted up in bed to find Simon still asleep on the floor. Gilbert was nowhere in the room. It was already 9am, Gilbert's shift ended two hours ago. I shook Simon awake and asked if he too could smell the burning. We followed the smell down the stairs.

My heart was pounding until we stopped at the kitchen door. Simon pushed open the door and began laughing. I peered over his shoulder to see smoke rising from the stove. Gilbert was trying to cook us breakfast. Nothing like a fully burnt English breakfast. Literally everything was burnt. I could swear even the orange juice was burnt.

We downed about as much burnt food as we could before heading to the library. Since Mr. Kunkle and Sampson couldn't find anything on their own we decided we should help.

A day at the library was unsuccessful once again. I had scanned books upon books in that damn library day after day and always came up short. I wasn't even sure what it was that we were looking for; maybe some kind of book on legends that describes what we were experiencing.

The days had been slow since the last bedroom ghostly occurrence. We had been keeping up the night shifts on our own, while Mr. Kunkle remained in his room alone. We had been seeing even less of Mr. Kunkle throughout the days. Mostly dinner time was the only time we ever spoke to him.

One night Mr. Kunkle said, "I am busy figuring all this out, if you need me, I will be there for you but until then I'll be in my study," in response to Simon asking about where he's been and how we've been doing nothing to help.

A tiny argument went on at dinner that night that ended in Mr. Kunkle leaving the room without another word. He had been right, nothing bad had happened for at least a week. So why should we worry if nothing was going on for the time being.

The next morning Mr. Kunkle had apologized to the three of us through a note placed on top of some strawberry danishes. It felt as if we should've been the ones to apologize; besides he was the one who was right. We caught Mr. Kunkle just before he left to get some milk from the store and apologized.

The peace, however, was short lived. That night, something happened. I had first shift until 2:00am. The best shift, you stay up late and get to sleep the rest of the night. Gilbert had the worst shift of the night, from 2 until 4:30. Just when you feel you've fallen fully asleep you get awoken to do the shift. Then you can sleep after that. A chunk of your sleep is taken out, and you can really feel it hit you in the morning- the lack of sleep.

Claire Hyatt

However the lack of sleep isn't what would be bothering Gilbert in the morning. That night while Simon and I slept and Gilbert kept watch, something happened.

The floor began to creak. Gilbert sat up in alert. He was prepared for any encounter. And that's when the nails began popping out of the floor boards. He thought he should've woken us up but he decided against it. The nails floated away and he could hear faint voices in the distance. Still staring at the floor board without nails, he got to his feet. The board lifted itself up. Gilbert trembled. He courageously took one step towards the hole. There was something inside the floor boards. It was a box of some sort. He turned to wake Simon and I, but we were no longer there.

Gilbert got up to run out of the room. The door slammed right in his face and he fell back.

Gilbert woke up on the sofa because I was shaking him. "You were supposed to be keeping watch!" Simon shouted to his brother.

"I-I-I was awake; I got hit by the- the door..." Gilbert stuttered, standing up. I gave him a funny look. "There's something underneath you!" He pointed to beneath my feet.

Confused, I moved towards him. I put my hands on his shoulders and sat him back on the sofa. "Now calmly explain what happened last night."

Gilbert explained to the best of his ability exactly what happened last night. He ended with, "I swear I'm not making this up! Please just check under the boards."

Simon and I exchanged a look, we both knew he had been dreaming, but what if there really was something under the floor boards. "There could be something useful down there, we may as well try." Simon said. Gilbert smiled.

"Well we're not getting any younger," I stated, "let's go get some tools."

Despite the fact that it was roughly five in the morning, we tore up those floor boards. Strangely enough, right where Gilbert had said, there was a box. The box had an old rusty lock on it, which was easily broken with a single hit from a hammer. The box was wooden on the outside and covered in dust. Inside the box lay two items. "Maybe we should get Mr. Kunkle", Gilbert said, looking towards Simon. Simon shook his head and pulled the two items out of the box.

One item was a key, old and rusted with three small engraved numbers on it *347*. I was dumbfounded as to what this key could potentially open; there were so many locks in the house.

The second object was a book. Simon held onto the book for quite some time and Gilbert just stared blankly at it. "What is that?" I asked pointing towards the book.

"I'm not sure, but it looks extremely familiar." Gilbert replied. Simon looked up at us and then back to the book. He opened his mouth to speak, but said nothing.

I looked to Gilbert questioningly, but Gilbert offered no answers. We stood behind Simon as he opened the book. The first page in the book read

Journal

Name: *Betty-Anne*

Simon dropped the book right back in the hole. He stood there numb with confusion. Then he spoke "I think we should go get Mr. Kunkle now."

I agreed, reaching to pick up the journal out of the hole. I stood back up and dusted it off as Simon, Gilbert and I walked to Mr. Kunkle's room.

Claire Hyatt

Chapter Sixteen

Mr. Kunkle was not in his room however. Why Mr. Kunkle was with Sampson in his study at six in the morning was beyond me, but that question was not important. Mr. Kunkle appeared to be just as confused as the rest of us as to why Betty-Anne's (the girl who fell off the balcony and died) journal would be in the floor boards in Simon's room.

I picked at my fingernails as Mr. Kunkle decided what we should do. "Maybe you'll find some clues in amongst this journal, go to the library and start reading, I'll be right there with some breakfast."

As we made our way to the library, Gilbert and I shared looks of remorse for Simon. Simon's face held no emotion, he just looked empty. I bet that's how he felt as well, empty.

All this talk about Betty-Anne's death probably brought up a lot of pushed away feelings. It's like her journal was forcing him to relive her last moments. His wounds were still fresh; it had only been a two years since her passing.

In the library the three of us sat on the Victorian fainting couch that was against one of the windows. We left the hard chair for Mr. Kunkle when he arrived. We sat in muteness for a few minutes until Simon spoke, "I think Mr. Kunkle said that we should start reading," he looked down at the floor, "this could mean something, everything happens for a reason."

Gilbert opened to the first page of her entries. The first entry was September 28th 2011.

It read: *I don't know what's going on. Something weird is happening here and I feel there is no one to tell. I can sense something evil. It has been lurking around the mansion for a while now. What am I to do? Perhaps Simon could help me figure it all out, oh but what if he gets hurt? I must do this on my own and tell the others when the time is right. Until I can tell anyone, I must express myself through this journal....*

Simon's face got a little bit flushed and he swallowed with difficulty. "This is exactly how she would say it too if she were talking." A tear escaped his eye and we continued reading.

Claire Hyatt

The next few entries were pointless; Betty-Anne was just confused, she had no answers. Over the course of five months and 10 entries there was no further information. It wasn't until March 19th that one entry caught our eye.

I think I have finally figured it all out. I could be at a breakthrough in my work. I have been having a hard time keeping this all from Simon but maybe I can finally tell him. The key is the spirits. They are the connection to this all. I read in our library this has happened one other time in history. These spirits are connected with……

The next page was ripped out. And so were the next eight pages. Mr. Kunkle came in with tea and some biscuits with jam. We ate as he read up to the entry before the pages disappeared. He took out his reading glasses that magnified his eyes to look as big as his head. He had an inquisitive look in his eyes as if the glasses helped him read between the lines. "She definitely knew something we don't, if only we had the next few pages."

Simon decided we should read the next entry that wasn't ripped out.

April 28th 2011,

It all makes sense now. I ~~must~~ can't tell Simon. It's too dangerous. I can't put him and the others in this kind of danger. Maybe Mr. Kunkle would understand, or maybe he would send us all away. This is not good. What am I to do? This kind of knowledge for a 15 year-old is not good. Maybe I should forget it all and let fate play out the way it should.

May 2nd 2011,

I've tried to forget and ignore it all, it's not working. HE has found out I know. I can't know. What will HE do to me? I'm too young to die. I've decided to hide all my knowledge, but I mustn't forget. I have been much too secretive lately, if Simon finds out I've been keeping all of this a secret, he will be so disappointed.

"More pages are gone," I said aloud to no one in particular. All four of us had squeezed onto the loveseat our eyes big and curious. Simon was still choking down his sobs as his name was continually mentioned. It wasn't until the entry of July 10th that everything seemed to come together.

Claire Hyatt

The page had been ripped out for whatever reason, but since there had been no writing on the following pages we were able to see the imprint of what had been written. I ran to the study, grabbed a pencil. When I returned to the library I had Mr. Kunkle shade over the imprinted paper.

I don't know how this will play out when I'm gone but it must be done. My existence is only going to harm the people I love. I don't know how to say goodbye to everyone. I've been such a silly girl doing the things I've done. I should've just ignored HIM altogether. If I did, I wouldn't be writing this. I'm scared, I never planned any of this. Today, I am going to die. I am ready. It has to be done. I'm sorry Mr. Kunkle, I should've said something sooner, and maybe I could've put a stop to it all. It's like I've made a bet with the devil and I lost. I'm sorry to everyone I could hurt by doing this. I wish I could have my best friend by my side in all of this. If Simon, you ever read this, you must know it is not your fault. I had to take my own life. I'm going to jump off the balcony. This is the only way to keep you all safe. I love you all, this is goodbye.

By the end of her entry we all had lumps in our throats. We were silent. I didn't know what to say. Those torn out entries took away the only chance of deciphering why Betty-Anne had done what she did. The library was filled with sorrow. It felt more quiet than usual. That was her last entry.

As Gilbert went to close the book Simon stopped him. "Wait, there's something we're missing. There is more writing on the very last page."

Gilbert flipped to the last page, and sure enough there was writing, only it wasn't from Betty-Anne.

Claire Hyatt

Chapter Seventeen

 *Simon,*

If you find this, just know we're sorry. We did this to protect ourselves and you. What you were doing looking under your floorboards is beyond us, however if you're looking for answers you won't find them here. You and Gilbert were so focused on B.A's death that you didn't find her journal first. What we found out should never be talked about. We disposed of the harmful evidence that B.A discovered. She was a smart girl, almost too smart. Her smarts are what led to her death. Her smarts are what forced us to leave. Please, don't do anything stupid.

With love,

Paul   *Emily*   Paige

Darla   Jacky   Karl

Our jaws dropped. "The-they knew..." Simon stammered.

"Bloody hell!" Gilbert exclaimed. I felt a pit of anger in my stomach. They just left them here without any knowledge, how could they.

"I can't believe my eyes." Mr. Kunkle sighed.

"They knew," Simon repeated, "they knew Betty-Anne killed herself, and they just left me thinking it was my fault she fell. How-how could they?"

"I thought they were our friends. They thought they were protecting us? From what? They let me believe..." Simon's rage died out. His anger turned to tears.

The people he thought were his best friends betrayed him. Simon left in tears. He ran to his room. Mr. Kunkle was just silent. I felt he should've said something in reassurance, but he didn't. After a while Mr. Kunkle got up and left.

Gilbert and I remained in the library alone. "I think you should go talk to him" I said. Gilbert nodded. He stood up and left me alone in the library.

I sat on the loveseat alone with the journal and my thoughts. My thoughts then led me to Mr. Kunkle's study where the key was placed. The key! That was it, I figured it out. Without another thought I grabbed the key and ran to Simon's room.

I walked in silently and Simon was talking in between sobs. He sounded so hurt and I knew how to help clear up the betrayal. "They didn't do it to hurt you Simon, they were protecting us," Gilbert said trying to reason.

"They knew everything, they just left us with a damn journal, they're no help and we're going to die. I hate them." Maybe Simon was overreacting a bit, but he was entitled to be angry. He wiped his tears when he saw me and that's when I spoke up.

"The key," was all I said at first, "The key is the key." Gilbert and Simon both stared blankly. They were probably thinking, 'what the heck is she talking about.' So I held up the key and continued talking. "Whatever this unlocks, could be the key to this whole mess. Maybe they hid the other pages in there. Your friends put this in there for a reason."

I think I had just turned the tides. Simon looked up, fixing his glasses. He looked as if he just had an epiphany.

"Maybe you're right. They were looking out for us after all!"

I really hope I was right with my theory, or it would just hurt Simon even more in the end.

We began searching for locked doors and trunks and any possible thing that a key could potentially open. The first place we could think of was the basement. "Uh ladies first," Gilbert said smiling.

"Noo way, you can go first," I said nudging him.

"I'll go first," Simon said. He was so determined to find this key hole I was sure he'd risk his life to find it. So down the stairs Simon went. He held his head high and didn't care whether we followed or not.

The truth is we were so curious we followed right behind, not thinking to bring any candle or flashlight down with us. It was really dark and even though no young girls were down there with us, something still felt a little off.

Simon fidgeted with his hands in the air to find the pull-cord. He then clicked on the light and the basement dimly lit up. There were empty boxes everywhere, covered in years of dust. The smell of mildew was still very strong.

There was a crawl space underneath the stairs. Gilbert said it smelt like rotting meat under there but he still crawled in. Upon returning he stated there was nothing but a dirty old toy train. I smiled, although I don't know why. My experience with the toy train hadn't been a good one.

We must have searched in all those boxes. In each and every box we came up short. There was however, a music box on top of an old singer foot driven sewing machine, but the key was no fit. I was surprised that we had been down there at least three hours without any paranormal experience. I guess when you're busy you seem to lose track of time.

There might have been like two boxes we missed but we were pretty certain there was nothing that could help us in that basement. Thinking about it further, I came to the conclusion that the other kids, being scared of their knowledge wouldn't go down into the creepy moldy, rotting basement to hide something.

Just when the three of us were about to go back upstairs, the door opened. Simon had already clicked the dim light off, so we were in total darkness. "Uh, Mr. Kunkle?" Gilbert called up the stairs. No answer. So Gilbert repeated himself.

"You kids shouldn't be down here," it was the familiar voice of Sampson. I let out a breath of relief. We made our way up the stairs and followed Sampson into the dining room. "So what were you doing down there for so long?" Sampson asked.

"We were just looking around," I said, unsure if I should bring up the key, seeing as how I just took it from Mr. Kunkle's office. Sampson stared at the three of us, questioning our motives.

"You shouldn't be searching for answers to those questions, you might not like what you find," was all he said before disappearing.

Just then Mr. Kunkle walked in holding a tray of various sandwiches- egg salad, roast beef, and tuna. "You're just in time for supper, you must all be hungry. I didn't see you get lunch."

We ate and ate. My stomach was so full. During supper there was minimal small talk. You could tell Mr. Kunkle was avoiding conversation about that morning and Betty-Anne's journal.

Before bed Simon, Gilbert and I discussed how we would search for what the key unlocks. "We should make our way up, since we've already checked the entire basement." Gilbert whispered.

"I think Gilbert is right, we should check the first floor tomorrow. It could take a few days, then we'll check the second floor, and after that we can check the third floor and the attic." Simon whispered back. We agreed and then drifted off, except for Simon who had first night duty.

The next day was a bust when Mr. Kunkle sent us to go get groceries; he said that Sampson wanted to show him how to make a delicious variation of Ploughman's Lunch.

The day after that was also unproductive when Sampson sent us to the library to find a book that he had said would help us. He wanted us to find "The Ghost in the Machine" claiming it could solve all of our problems. Sampson really pushed the idea that this book could be very helpful. Simon, Gilbert and I respected Sampson's wishes. We tore through as many books as we could, searching for the one Sampson had mentioned.

Mr. Kunkle came and found us around lunchtime. "I have discussed the entire situation with Sampson and he greatly believes that this can help us. I know it's a lot of work and the library is big, but please if you could find it, we would both greatly appreciate it."

After lunch I got a call from my parents who were checking up on me and then we continued our search in the library. From one row to another we searched. At this point my eyes were sore and I was really beginning to despise the person who didn't think it would be a good idea to put the books in alphabetical order.

Each bookshelf had three sections, with at least twenty books on each. The library was huge; I would say it had at least 60 book shelves, give or take a few. That rounds out to about 3,600 books which leaves roughly 1,200 for each of us. One day was not enough. My back was aching from bending over to read the book titles. Many of the binds of the old books were brown and torn so I couldn't read the titles properly, this made me have to take out at least half of the books just to read the front cover.

I subconsciously kept a list in my head of all the books I wished to return to so I could read them. The books that really caught my eye were the series of old folk tales. Not only were the stories old, but the actual books themselves. The leather blue outsides had been frayed and covered in layers of dust.

Three days and 3,600 books later, the three of us stopped our search. We had not found the book Sampson had wanted. We had wasted three days. Three days that could've been used to find a key hole.

We all slumped up the stairs, feeling deflated, to Mr. Kunkle's study to tell him we couldn't find it. Upon arriving in his office we noticed that there was a book underneath one of the arm chairs. This was very unusual because Mr. Kunkle always kept everything neat and tidy. I greeted Mr. Kunkle and walked over the lone arm chair to go pick up the book.

It wasn't until I was handing the book to Mr. Kunkle that I realized what the book was.

"Ah you've found it I see!" Mr. Kunkle looked satisfied, "I really hope this will be able to help us, thank you so much." I looked back to him in confusion. How could he have not known it was there? "Is there something wrong Aria?"

I shook my head and pulled Gilbert and Simon into the hallway, giving Mr. Kunkle a polite goodbye wave.

Claire Hyatt

Chapter Eighteen

"The book has been in his study the entire time, and he didn't even notice." I whispered.

"But that just doesn't make sense, how could he not see the book there?" Simon responded.

"I don't know," I answered, "but it might have something to do with Samps-" I was cut off by Gilbert who nudged me quite hard. Sampson was now standing right behind me. I turned to face Sampson. Blushing, I took a step back, "Good day Sampson." I smiled, nodded my head and turned the corner. Once I passed the corner I ran all the way down the hallway. I ended my nice little jog at the bottom of the grand staircase. Simon and Gilbert weren't far behind me.

"That was bad," I noted once I regained my breath.

Gilbert nodded, "I think we should just forget the whole thing and go search for this key's hole." He held up the key. Determined as we were, we did forget Sampson's wild goose chase and began to search the first floor.

As I searched the drawers of the kitchen I was once again reminded of how strange the mansion had been lately. I looked out the window to where Coraline's row of trees had once been. It was then that I realized I had not seen or experienced a single paranormal thing for about a week, besides Sampson. The house used to be filled with the dead; it was crowded with spirits to the point where the house felt stuffy. Now it was as if they all decided to get up and walk away one day. Almost as if on cue something happened.

One of the oak cupboard doors creaked open slowly. I quickly turned my head to the source of the noise. Practically simultaneously Gilbert shouted to me from the dining room about some chipped piece of china while the door to the basement swung open crashing against wall. I held my head to try and focus for a second. I didn't care about broken china or a dusty cupboard with plastic bowls so I turned to face the creaky old stairs to the basement.

A rush of hot air came up from downstairs and blew through my hair. My hair entangled itself and rested over my face. I hesitated to move my hair, scared of what I might see. With uneasy breaths I reached my hand up and brushed my bangs out of my eyes. Thankfully there was nothing standing in front of me. All of a sudden I felt the same warm air on my neck. The air urged me closer to the stairs. I took one step before peering down into the dark basement. I stared into the darkness. It took a while for my eyes to register what was down the stairs. I could see a dark figure lurking right at the bottom of the stairs. It was watching me. The warm air urged me one more time. I took another step.

Just then the door slammed shut and a shout of anger escaped the closing door. Gilbert was standing in front of the closed door. "What the hell were you looking at?!" he asked, "You were standing there for like five minutes."

I shook my head trying to regain my thoughts, "I'm not quite sure, but I don't think I'm going down in the basement again anytime soon. There was someone down there."

"At least that thing wasn't down there when we were hey ahahah," Gilbert said jokingly, although his laugh seemed to be forced. Gilbert sounded a bit nervous. I sure hope that thing wasn't down there. Why would that thing try to lure me into the basement alone? I shook my head again and shrugged my shoulders.

"Oh well, let's just forget about it. Did you find anything in the dining room?"

"Nope, nothing but some broken china bowls, no key is fitting in there," he smiled, a little bit proud of his joke, "I don't assume you found anything in here either?" I ignored his question because the answer was quite obvious as we made our way to the parlor to go see if Simon had discovered anything.

The parlor was just down the right corridor past the library. The hallway was long like hotels and had seashell wallpaper covering the walls. I followed the red carpet to the open door where Simon was.

The parlor was lovely, except for its musty smell. If the library didn't have so many books and open space, the parlor would be my favourite. The walls were covered in textured cream wallpaper that contrasted perfectly with the walnut table in the center of the room. Five red Victorian armchairs were scattered around the room; two at the table and three in the corners. The glass chandelier emitted a little glow of orangey light. Taking up most of the east wall was a beautiful cast iron fireplace with decorative surround of swirls and flowers. The mantel on top held old black and white photographs of random people I'd never know.

Simon was bent over a roll-top desk in one corner looking in one of the various drawers. He stood up brushed off his dusty knees and shook his head. "I've found nothing all day, I already checked across the hall in the billiard room, nothing there either."

I sighed, "Well they didn't build Rome in a day. We'll try again tomorrow."

A week went by and the entire first floor had been rummaged. I was starting to get a little discouraged but Gilbert and Simon had all the positivity in the world. "Two floors down, two to go!" They'd say. Gilbert's favourite line was, "Well now I know where that is."

Another week passed of nothingness. We'd been searching everywhere – bathrooms, closets, trunks, cupboards. Anywhere anything could potentially be we would look. We had lost two days during the week because we needed a break and someone had to eventually go get groceries. The first floor was larger which is why it took like ten days; the second floor wouldn't take nearly that much time. We had almost finished searching the entire second floor. There were roughly ten rooms left, which we could do in a day.

Claire Hyatt

Chapter Nineteen

Simon had made a list of all the rooms in the house. We checked off the rooms we had finished. At first I felt that the list was discouraging because it showed how many rooms we had left, but then I remembered that Mom always told me to be optimistic. The list was to show our progress not what still had to be done. I would say we were making pretty good progress.

Simon waited for the chance to check Mr. Kunkle's office while Gilbert searched the drawing room just down the hall. I looked over the list and noticed that we had failed to search two bedrooms in the North end of the home. Since the North end was on the other side of the mansion I left Simon with the key and told him where I was going. I took the list with me.

I walked right into the little boy with the train as I turned down the small corridor. I decided not to stick around and watch his face fall off again so I carefully walked around him as he stared at me.

As I made my way to the two rooms, one across from the other, I chose to go to the one on the left first. I instantly regretted my decision when a rush of dizziness hit me once I entered the room. I reached for the dusty old wooden armchair for support and took in my surroundings. I suddenly understood why this room had not been searched. Pink flowered wallpaper covered the walls. A pale pink carpet made its place underneath the poster bed. Dust covered everything; it looked like no one had been here in forever. A porcelain doll sat on top of the bed with the initials BA on the pink porcelain shoe. This was Betty-Anne's bedroom.

I quickly felt queasy. I looked out the window to the balcony and thought of Betty-Anne's last moments. She must have been so scared. She must have felt totally alone. I couldn't even begin to imagine what was going through her head.

I stopped leaning on the chair for support and began to rummage the room. I searched the most obvious places first; under the bed, in the closet, in the drawers. Searching this room felt different, I felt like I was invading the room of someone who was still alive. I sensed as if I shouldn't be there. Just then the faded pink curtains began to blow. In with the wind came the strong smell of lilacs. The smell was so strong I was beginning to get a headache. I debated taking a step out on the balcony for fresh air but my subconscious decided against it and I continued searching the room.

I had now felt as if I had searched almost the entire room, but just to be sure I checked under the carpet. After finding nothing but a few dust bunnies I stood up and stretched my back. I reached my arms towards the ceiling and arched my back so far I heard a crack. It felt so delightful to stretch after bending over for so long.

I was just about to leave the room when I felt a friendly hand rest on my shoulder. I shivered. The hand pushed harder guiding me to the corner of the room. I stood looking at the pink wallpaper when the hand released its pressure. I was completely alone in the room. I felt no more presences. I was led to that corner for a reason.

I scanned the pink wall, looking up, down and side to side. Nothing seemed out of the ordinary. Just as I was turning around to leave, something caught my eye. A dark shadow was in my peripheral view. I stopped, turning only my head to look at the shadow. The shadow transcended across the wall, disappearing right in the corner. I bent down to investigate where this shadow disappeared, that was when I noticed a rip in the wallpaper.

The corner of wallpaper had been folded up revealing a dark wood. I pinched the end of the wallpaper and pulled it back just a bit. More wood was exposed. I had a hunch about this wall and knocked quietly twice on the wood. My knock echoed behind the wall further than it should have. This wall was hollow.

I grabbed at the wallpaper once more and began peeling it upwards. More wood went all the way up the wall for about four feet, and then it turned into a plain white wall. I then began to pull sideways, for another 2 feet it was wood, then wall. I ripped off all the wall paper that was covering the wood. I stood back and observed the wall. I gasped. "Oh my--" I ran straight out of the room as fast as I could. I sprinted down the thin corridor and right into Mr. Kunkle's office.

Simon wasn't in there, so I apologized to Mr. Kunkle for the interruption. "Simon and Gilbert are in the drawing room."

"Okay, thanks!" I closed the door behind me and dashed to the drawing room.

I was out of breath when I entered the room, "Come, *huff*, I found, *huff*, bring the key…" I guess they understood what I was trying to say as they both jumped up.

I led them towards the North end running as fast as I could. My stomach tightened at the thought that what I saw wouldn't be there anymore. I stopped in front of the door to Betty-Anne's room, not remembering that I had closed it.
I reached for the silvery door knob and turned slowly. I looked back at Simon and Gilbert, they both breathed heavily. Simon was hesitant to enter the room, and when he did I heard his throat choke up his words. "Look," I pointed to the corner.

Gilbert and Simon both gasped. "Bloody hell!" Gilbert exclaimed.

"Holy moly! This was not here before!" Simon puffed out, observing the door. The dark wooden door in the corner looked like a closet door for hobbits. I reached out and the knob wouldn't budge. Just above the knob was a tiny key hole. I took a step back and looked towards Simon, who was holding the key.

Simon's shaky hand stretched out to the key hole. We all leaned our heads in. My heart beat so loud I thought Simon and Gilbert would be able to hear it. Simon put the key into the key hole, and he slowly turned it to the right. Suspense was eating at all of us. He continued to turn the key. Suddenly we heard a click.

Simon turned to look at Gilbert and I, his smile was so big and there were tears in his eyes. There were tears in all of our eyes. Instantly we all grabbed each other and began screaming, "It's a fit! The key fit!"

Our happiness was so overwhelming that I had to start wiping tears from my cheeks. "No sense waiting, let's open it." Gilbert said. With the key still in the lock Simon slowly opened the door. It was pitch black; you couldn't see how far back it went or if there was anything in it. "I'll go get some light." Gilbert hurried out of the room. He came back a few short minutes later holding two candles, a match box and an old flashlight. "This is the best I could do," he said smiling.

I quickly struck one match and lit my white candle. I used the fire on my candle to light Simon's as well. Gilbert flicked on the flashlight which quickly flicked back off, he sighed. The old batteries had died. "That's okay," I said, "These candles should emit enough light in there."

I ducked my head to get in the door as I followed behind Simon and Gilbert. The candles produced just enough light to be able to see our surroundings. To our surprise we were all able to stand up, only the doorway was small. We were in what looked like a walk in closet, or storage space. There were boxes scattered on the ground covered in layers of dust. In finding the walls around us we discovered paintings covering the walls. "These were our adventures," Simon piped up. Betty-Anne was a great painter and she was very smart too.

The back wall was full of drawings. These weren't just any kind of drawings, this was a timeline. Betty-Anne was plotting out the seers who died. She connected names with other names and cities. It was almost a pyramid of sorts. At the top of the pyramid was a question mark. The second in line for the pyramid was a shocking name with a question mark beside it. I stood on my tippy-toes to get a better look at the name because I didn't believe what the wall said or why. I gasped. The wall read, "Sampson?"

Just then our candles blew out. We were in pitch black again. Trying to remember where the door was I stumbled into Gilbert who tripped over a box. Simon stood still in one corner; he could hear heavy breathing in his ear and felt warm breath on his neck.

"L-let's get outta here!" I shouted. When did the door close? I thought to myself. I felt around the wall searching for a door knob, I found none. Beneath my fingertips I felt the cool wall switch into a rough patch, this was where the door was.

I grabbed Gilbert and called out to Simon who followed my voice to the door. The three of us banged on the door loudly, shouting for help. After pounding on the door I heard a pain staking scream, and then the three of us toppled out the doorway onto the floor. I brushed my bangs out of my eyes and rolled off of Gilbert. His eyes were big and scared. Simon lay on the ground beside me, his hands on his head.

I wiped off my dusty knees and stood up. I helped Gilbert off the ground first. Simon went to stand when he realized he had no pants on. His pants were in a pile on the ground split entirely in half. His eyes got wide, and his face turned pink as he noticed he was wearing his spaceship boxer briefs.

"Find what you were looking for?"

Sampson stood in the doorway followed by Mr. Kunkle. "We heard some noises and Sampson said he knew where you were" Mr. Kunkle explained. "Just making sure you're okay." He turned to leave, "Oh and Simon, please put some pants on." Simon went even redder.

After Sampson and Mr. Kunkle left, Gilbert grabbed my arm and swung me around to face the room. "I-I don't understand," he said, "Where's the door?"

I studied the wall from a distance before walking closer to the pink wallpapered walls. "This isn't even physically possible," Simon said, "It can't just disappear."

I was so confused. I reached down into the corner to check the wallpaper. There was no rip. I decided to make my own; there was no wood behind the wallpaper.

The three of us stood silently for quite some time staring at that pink flowered wall. My head hurt from trying to comprehend what had just happened. I couldn't make out anything. Nothing made sense. Why was Sampson's name in that closet? How does a door just disappear? And what happened to Simon's pants?

Simon was right; it's not physically possible for a door to be there and then just disappear. We had originally thought that finding the key's hole would solve all of our problems, but it just left us with many more unanswered questions.

That night none of us could sleep. Nobody talked but you could tell we were all lying awake staring at the ceiling based on our breathing patterns. We only talked when one of us had to switch to do night watch.

While I sat awake I thought about the talk I had with my parents earlier that night; they had said they wanted to come for a visit for my birthday next month. I really really wanted to see them, but I told them not to waste their money. I couldn't be so selfish as to put my need before my parents' safety. I reassured them I would be okay because Gilbert's birthday was only two days after mine and Simon was going to make us both a wonderful cake. I was lying about the cake of course. There would be no party or celebration until we figured everything out. My parents seemed to be pleased with my lies and so they agreed to stay home, wished me a good night and hung up.

In the morning I slugged down the hallway down the grand staircase right into the dining room. I nearly fell asleep in my porridge. I looked at myself in the spoon; my eyes had dark circles underneath them. I looked across the table to Gilbert; he too had bags under his eyes.

Simon looked tired as ever as he came into the dining room holding a tray with three steaming cups of tea. His red slippers dragged across the wooden floor, and one of them caught a nail that was sticking up out of the floor. He stumbled dropping the tray of tea.

Simon swore as the three tea cups shattered into tiny pieces. The loud shattering noise definitely woke us all up. I tiptoed around the broken china as I went to go get a broom. Poor Simon, his week just kept getting worse. I passed a sad Mr. Kunkle in the hallway as I went to get the broom in the closet by the telephone, he didn't speak at all. I knew exactly where the broom was, right beside the feather duster that hung on the wall above the blue bucket.

We cleaned up the mess without much work. I was sad to see my favourite purple flower tea cup thrown in the garbage but there was an entire collection of the same tea cups in different colours in the bottom cupboard.

"Hey did you guys see Mr. Kunkle yet?" I asked as we washed our breakfast dishes. "I saw him walking this way earlier, he looked upset."

"No we haven't seen him yet today, maybe we should go find him," Gilbert offered.

"Yes lets," Simon agreed. "We'll bring him tea as well. Gilbert can carry it this time." I smiled, happy that Simon could still make jokes.

I wasn't sure if Mr. Kunkle wanted any company because he looked so upset in the hallway, but maybe I just interpreted his body language wrong. I hope that was the case.

I was disappointed to find out that Mr. Kunkle was indeed upset. We found him alone in his study crying. Simon placed the brown tea cup on his desk and passed him a handkerchief. Mr. Kunkle blew his nose loudly in the handkerchief before straightening up and looking at us.

He turned back into 'professor' mode as he spoke, "My friend, my best friend, he was murdered last night. He was the last of my seer friends. There are so few of us left. I don't know what to do. But I know that I must go and investigate."

We looked at him with remorse. "I don't want your pity," Mr. Kunkle said, "it's just hard to lose all of your friends, I will be okay once I get back and straighten everything out. A cab will be here to get me tonight."

"Are you going to leave us here alone sir," I asked politely.

"I know it seems very irresponsible of me to leave at this time, but I must; besides Sampson will be here for you if you need anything at all. You can count on him."

I smiled trying to cover my doubt in his statement. I wasn't so sure about Sampson anymore, no matter how much of a help he has been.

If it would make Mr. Kunkle happy to go, I would respect his wishes. He would only be gone a few days. "Would you like us to help you pack?"

"That would be lovely thank you," replied Mr. Kunkle.

Claire Hyatt

Chapter Twenty

That evening when the cab pulled up we were all sad to say goodbye to Mr. Kunkle. We wished him the best on his trip and gave him our condolences for his loss. Mr. Kunkle stated "I haven't seen Sampson since last night, so if you could please let him know what's going on and tell him he is to take care of you it would be much appreciated."

"We certainly will, goodbye," Simon said as he closed Mr. Kunkle in the cab. The cab drove slowly out the gate and we stood by the gargoyles on the stairs until the cab was out of sight.

We had already had supper and dusk was approaching quickly. With little daylight we weren't quite sure what to do with ourselves. I decided to have a quick shower so that I wouldn't have to do it in the morning. Once out of the shower I got on my pajamas in my bedroom. My bedroom seemed to be foreign. It didn't feel like it was mine anymore. I was barely in my room, dust covered my dressers.

I walked out of my room and down the grand staircase just in time for some tea. I went to the kettle and poured out three cups of tea. Simon stood beside me with some cream for Gilbert's cup. Gilbert was in the library on the fainting couch with a new book in hand. I sat alone in the loveseat and Simon took a place on the lounge chair.

I was so comfy and warm in my silk pajamas. The earl grey tea warmed my hands. It felt so peaceful, it was almost as if we didn't have any problems and we weren't in danger. That is, until the spirit showed up.

He hovered just above the floor. He had gray hair, a very wrinkled face and a rough beard of white whiskers. His fingers were crooked and his teeth were yellowing. "On nadchodzi. Nie pozwól, Eugene zostawić, to nie jest bezpieczne," was all he said. He said it three times before disappearing.

"Uh, did anyone catch what he was saying?" I asked.

"No, I'm not even sure what language that was." Simon said

"That was anything but English." Gilbert stated.

Claire Hyatt

After about half an hour of pondering the strange man's words, we decided it was time for bed. During the night it stormed. It was the first thunder storm of the spring. The rain hit Simon's window with such power it was as if someone was throwing rocks. The lightning flashed bright yellow behind the blinds, quickly followed by loud rumbles of thunder. During my night watch I sat in the rocking chair by the window and watched the storm out the open window.

The warm spring breeze blew through my hair and I took deep breaths breathing in the smell of rain mixed with blossoms. The rain hit my face and my cheeks stung with every hard raindrop. I watched as another quick strike of lightning hit, immediately followed by a roar of thunder. The house shook. There was nothing in that moment that could trouble me. It was serene. People live for moments like that.

The storm began to pick up. The wind howled its way through the open window. I slowly slid the window shut and I began watching the storm through the glass. The loudest bit of thunder came at the exact time the lightning did. Simultaneously the town's lights in the distance all shut off. The power was out. The house was even quieter now without the constant buzz of electricity running through the walls. My night watch was over now. I fell asleep to the peaceful sound of rain pitter-pattering against the window pane.

In the morning the power was still off so we couldn't make our morning tea. For breakfast all we could have was some bread with strawberry jam.

Sampson was still nowhere to be found. I decided to go look for him on the second floor. I first went to Mr. Kunkle's study, and that's the only place I looked too. I got distracted by a picture on Mr. Kunkle's desk. Mr. Kunkle was standing in a green field with one other man. He had his hand on this man's shoulder. They were grinning. Mr. Kunkle was much younger in this picture, as was the other man. I knew I recognized the other male!

Regardless of the age difference, this man is the old man who visited us last night speaking in a foreign language. This picture was out on his desk for a reason. This was the last of Mr. Kunkle's seer friends to die. I wished I could've remembered what this man had said last night.

My wish must have been heard because that night when the three of us were having turkey sandwiches for dinner the man returned. "On nadchodzi. Nie pozwól, Eugene zostawić, to nie jest bezpieczne," he repeated over and over.

As soon as the man arrived Gilbert dashed out of the room and grabbed a paper and pen. He wrote to the best of his abilities what he believed this man to be saying. It wasn't much, but it was something. "Now we just need to know the language," Simon said.

"We'll do that tomorrow," I promised. "It's getting dark and the power is still out."

That night when we were settling down for bed I noticed that the town's lights were shining bright. "Hmm that's strange," I said to Gilbert, "we should go to the town tomorrow and see what's up."

When Simon came back in the room after brushing his teeth we blew out our candles and I drifted off to sleep.

That night I dreamt about living back in Ohio with my family and friends. In my dream Gilbert and Simon were my neighbours and they even had their parents living with them. They even had a dog named Mr. Kunkle. They seemed happy. It was a good dream. I couldn't remember the last time I had a good dream that wasn't a nightmare.

Claire Hyatt

Chapter Twenty-one

The next day when Gilbert and I told Simon about how the townspeople had power and we didn't, he told us we needed to find out what Mr. Kunkle's dead friend was telling us first. Simon said it could be crucial to our lives. Gilbert and I were well aware of Mr. Kunkle's friend's message, and the power could wait. The only time we really needed power was at night. We solved the tea problem by heating up the water on top of the fireplace. We only used the fire for tea because the weather was getting much warmer and there was no need for a fire anymore.

Simon and Gilbert began searching in the library for the language. They had only been searching a few minutes before I piped up, "How do you plan on finding the language? We're not going to find the words that you assumed he was saying on the first page of a book. You don't even know if you wrote it right."

Simon and Gilbert both stopped and stared at me. "I didn't mean to be discouraging. We could always go to the café in town and use their computer to search for it." I articulated.

The two boys looked at me as if I had two heads. I knew Mr. Kunkle wasn't interested in the world of internet, and he preferred paper but Mr. Kunkle wasn't here. I tried to reason with the two, who had obviously taken on Mr. Kunkle's mindset. I too admit that I began to think like Mr. Kunkle. I liked things old school now, except that damn rotary phone that I could never work.

We got on our shoes and headed out the door to the little café. Nobody had seen Sampson since the day we fell out of Betty-Anne's secret closet, so we didn't have to ask for permission to leave. I secretly put a few pounds in my pocket so I could buy us all some drinks. I didn't want the little old lady who owned Concord Café to think we were loitering. Once we stepped in the cooled café I walked towards the little old lady working the shop and asked for two green teas and one hazelnut vanilla coffee. She nodded and smiled through her wrinkles. I put the money on the counter before we turned to go to the computer. Simon and Gilbert didn't have much experience with the computer so I took over.

I knew exactly what website to go on. I always cheated on my Spanish homework with this translator website back in Ohio. If you enter some words it will detect the language and change it to whatever language you wish.

The little old lady brought us our drinks and offered us all freshly made shortbread cookies.

I typed in the words that Gilbert had handwritten on a piece of scrap paper into the online translator. The two boys were amazed as it translated the words I wrote. For the most part Gilbert did a pretty good job at understanding what the old man was saying because he was speaking an old form of Polish. The translation was: *HE is coming. Do not let Eugene leave, it is not safe.*

I choked on my coffee. Eugene is Mr. Kunkle's first name. We needed to get back to the mansion and fast; maybe we could find a phone number, or something. We needed to get a hold of Mr. Kunkle.

I left the little old lady a tip at our table, and we hurried out. I only stopped to ask her about the power. "Get Eugene to check your fuse box," she responded, "He's good with his hands." The old lady winked. I was a bit creeped out but there was no time for that. We bolted home as fast as we could.

Claire Hyatt

Chapter Twenty-two

The first place we could think to look would be Mr. Kunkle's study. He had to have some information on where his friend lived. Why didn't he tell us where he was going?

We were so focused on our mission to get to Mr. Kunkle's office that all three of us failed to notice the three crows sitting on one gargoyle at the top of the stairs. As we walked in the door we were greeted by the old man who got all up in our faces shouting "On nadchodzi. Nie pozwól, Eugene zostawić, to nie jest bezpieczne!" He stressed these words even more now before disappearing in a frustrated huff. This was not good at all.

Gilbert began making his way up the grand staircase when an old wicker wheelchair made its way out of the North end. The wheelchair creaked with every motion. There was no visible person guiding this wheelchair. It looked as if it was going to surpass the stairs, but it stopped dead center at the top. It creaked as it turned to face the stairs. Gilbert froze on the third step. The wheelchair backed up and hurled itself at Gilbert.

Gilbert fell backwards as the force of the wicker wheelchair hit him. The wheelchair fell apart at the impact. I rushed over to go help him. Thankfully he was fine. He walked it off as the three of us cautiously made our way up the stairs.

We turned to the left to where Mr. Kunkle's office was. A bit further down the hallway were our bedrooms. My bedroom door was open and so was Gilbert's which was directly across from mine. A baby carriage made its way from my bedroom to Gilbert's as slowly as possible. Then our doors both slammed making us all jump.

My heart was beating extremely fast. Suddenly the entire house began to shake viciously. I leaned against the wall for support but the house was shaking too much. We couldn't stay on our feet. We fell into a pile on the floor.

Once the house stopped shaking I tried to get up. I pushed off the wall to stand and all of a sudden an overwhelming smell of roses hit me. I had to sit on the ground with my back to the wall for support. Gilbert and Simon could smell it too. The smell of roses was so strong it gave me a headache and made my eyes water.

The smell remained for quite some time. Only after the smell vanished could any of us get off the floor. I felt so vulnerable on the ground, especially after the wheelchair and baby carriage. Who knows what else could have been lurking in the house.

I built up all the courage I had to turn and open Mr. Kunkle's office door, secretly hoping Sampson wouldn't be ka-clinking around inside. The room was empty, and everything was in right place. Sampson couldn't have been here, he would've moved something. Just then the door slammed shut. We all jumped and turned to face the door. "That's new," Gilbert said pointing out a note stuck to the back of the door. The note was in messy handwriting that was hard to make out. It read;

Please turn on the fuse box

-S

"Uh that's sketchy, a note from Sampson." I said to Gilbert and Simon.

"I don't think we should do it – trust Sampson - not after what we found in B.A's secret room," Simon said.

"That means nothing. We don't know what any of that is. I wouldn't mind a little light at night, especially after that wheelchair." Gilbert argued. I didn't quite agree with Gilbert's statement. We hadn't seen Sampson since that day. Yet I felt drawn to the basement. My curiosity shouldn't have superseded my fear, but it did.

"Mr. Kunkle wouldn't appreciate it when he comes home and all the food has gone bad and we have no power." I reasoned. "It doesn't mean we have to go down right this second, besides its getting dark, so let's just go down tomorrow morning."

Simon reluctantly agreed. It was getting dark awfully early considering summer was approaching and the days were supposed to be getting longer.

We left Mr. Kunkle's office after finding no sign of where he had gone. I was getting stressed out; his spirit friend had scared me. But Mr. Kunkle had gone away before and always returned days after. He was dealing with the last of his friends' deaths and he needed some time. He would be fine.

I slept restlessly all night paranoid about going down to the basement in the morning. There was no reason to be scared, I told myself. We had spent a day down there already and there was nothing down there. We would be fine, Mr. Kunkle is fine and everything will be all good. I did a poor job of convincing myself.

My Mom had taught me how to self-talk for when I started feeling extreme feelings and it wasn't working this time. My gut had originally told me just to go down there and that's why I convinced Gilbert and Simon, but my gut was now making me regret my decision. I had completely forgot that there was indeed something in the basement trying to lure me down when I was searching the kitchen for the key's hole.

Chapter Twenty-three

In the morning I awoke from a long tiring night. My eyes felt heavy and I could not work up an appetite. I pushed back my feelings and ate a slice of bread.

"Well, let's get this over with, it won't take long." I said, trying to convince myself to go through with it. I often wondered what Gilbert and Simon were thinking about our situation but their constant deep breaths confirmed that they were just as frightened. Hopefully we could just go downstairs, turn on the fuse box, come upstairs and get on with our lives. With our luck, that wasn't the case.

Armed with flashlights in our hands and shoes on our feet we made our way into the kitchen. I tied my hair back and out of my face, feeling the scar the broken mirror had left on my upper lip. My stomach was tight and full of butterflies. I noticed Gilbert's hands shaking as he tried to put new batteries in his flashlight. Simon lingered quietly behind us breathing quick fast breaths.

I looked to both of them and nodded. "Here goes nothing."

Gilbert's shaky hands reached out and touched the cold door knob. He grasped the knob and slowly turned to the right. He pulled the door back as Simon and I strained our necks to see down the creaky staircase. Dust floated out the open doorway and swirled around our heads. I swallowed before taking one step towards the stairs. Gilbert put his hand in front of me to stop me. "I'll go first," he smiled. I could tell he forced his smile. He was scared.

Simon followed behind me and the three of us made our way down the creaky wooden stairs just like we had done the first time. This time was different though, there were no little girls waiting for us at the bottom of the stairs. We didn't know what awaited us.

Gilbert flicked on his flashlight first, once the light from the kitchen faded away. Simon and I quickly turned ours on as well. "The fuse box should be in that corner," I said pointing to my right. I hope I remembered correctly from when we searched down here. I didn't want to send us in the wrong direction.

I followed behind the two of them to the corner. The dust in the basement thickened the air. I released breath I didn't know I was holding when I saw Gilbert's flashlight scan over a metal box in the corner.

Quickly in and out, safe and sound, I thought to myself as Gilbert opened the fuse box door. Gilbert held Simon's flashlight as Simon looked for the correct switch. With steady breaths Simon clicked off one switch and then right back on. A silent buzz returned to the house and a rush of relief washed over all of us. "That worked out well," Gilbert said, "now let's get the hell out of this damn basement."

"I don't think so", said an unfamiliar deep voice.

"What?" Gilbert asked; I repeated the "what" and so did Simon. We began frantically shining our flashlights around the basement. My flashlight scanned over a tall dark figure.

"Shit," I mumbled under my breath. "It's HIM," I whispered to Gilbert and Simon, "over there by the stairs. I know it's HIM."

We froze with our flashlights shining at the figure. I didn't know what to do. I could feel the adrenaline pumping through my veins but I still couldn't move. In this moment of decision the best thing you can do is the right thing; the worst thing you can do is nothing. The only thing I could think of in this moment was flashbacks of my childhood. My parents taking me to the park. When I got stung by a bee. Learning to ride a bike. My first friend. When I got my first pet. All these thoughts raced in my mind; memories, voices of people I knew, sounds of things I loved. My mother's voice rang loudest in my head, "I believe in you. I know you are strong and smart. You can do this. Stay focused, think positive and you will beat this."

I straightened my back. I refused to be scared. Who is HE that I'm going to give up my power to him. "Who are you and what do you want?" I demanded. Gilbert and Simon looked at me surprised. The figure stepped forward. Gilbert and Simon took a step back, I held my ground. The figure began laughing a deep maniacal laugh. Did he think I was humoring him? "I don't fear you."

"Nor I you," HE answered with an extremely deep voice. I choked on air. The sound of his voice was bloodcurdling.

"Here to kill us you coward?" I egged him on. I don't know what I was thinking, was I trying to get myself killed.

"No you fool; I leave the dirty work to the others." He instantly responded.

The other ghosts; he gets them to kill the seers. But why? I had to keep talking cocky so he would continue responding. "Making deals hey, 'cause you're not strong enough to kill us yourself." Gilbert tried to pull me back with him but I pulled out of his reach.

"Ha-ha, I could kill you right now," my breath caught as he spoke, "but then of course I wouldn't receive your power. I wouldn't build myself up. One day I will be strong enough."

I was petrified, but I had him right where I wanted him. "Who are you?" Simon stepped forward demanding. Good for him for speaking up, but he interfered with what I was getting at.

"I know you. Your little friend found me first. She was smart, but not smart enough. I didn't even have to get another ghost to kill her, she did it for me. And I received her powers and she passed on, just as promised," He smirked. He was playing with Simon's emotions.

Gilbert wouldn't let this idiot mess with his older brother, he stepped forward. "I know you. Your little pathetic life wasn't enough. So now you've come back to mess with everyone in the afterlife and you still have no friends. You're the fool." I don't know where Gilbert came up with that, and it sounded pretty harsh, but he didn't get in HIS head yet.

"That's cute, you think you know all. You all know nothing. Don't make me do something you'll regret. Go upstairs to those worthless lives of yours. I'm not done with you yet. I will be back, and I will be stronger. I'll take pleasure in killing you three on my own." The dark tall figure moved out of the way of the stairs. I wasn't sure I trusted turning my back while going up the stairs but my adrenaline wouldn't allow me to die.

"I'd like to see you try." Gilbert said as we pulled him up the stairs. I had never seen Gilbert like this before. He was a whole new person. He shouldn't have been so cocky though. We're all lucky we didn't get ourselves killed.

In that moment I was just glad to breathe cleaner air and see light. I didn't think of the fact that HE was in the house.

I didn't think of where we were going to go or how we were going to survive. I looked out the kitchen window once we closed and locked the basement door. "That's strange," I said quietly, my voice was still a little shaky. A horse and buggy were making their way up the driveway.

We ran to the front door to wait for whoever was here. I brushed the dust out of Simon's hair as we prepared to act somewhat normal for our visitor. When no knock came I got suspicious and I opened the door just as Mr. Kunkle was walking up the corroding stairs.

I was so thrilled to see Mr. Kunkle, I wanted to run up and give him a hug but I refrained from doing that because it would seem weird.

"Mr. Kunkle, we are so glad you're back! You'll never guess what just happened." Simon said.

"I can only stay for a while and then I must be on my way. Please Aria, put the kettle on." Mr. Kunkle said. I did as asked and came back with his favourite tea.

"I know you might think you know what's going on now, but you don't. I can see in all of your faces that you have seen HIM. But I assure you, it is not what you think. It is much much worse." He continued, "I really must be on my way, and as hard as it is for me to admit it, you must not trust Sampson anymore. He is not who you think he is. Don't let him in."

After a short tea Mr. Kunkle was back out the door. He told us he didn't know when he would be back and we should probably all just go to our homes.

He slowly got in to the buggy. The horse neighed and before we knew it, he was gone. We stood together for a long while on the stairs staring out to the rolling hills. "Wait a minute, what's this?" Gilbert asked, "I didn't know we got mail."

In one of the gargoyles' mouths was a newspaper clipping. Gilbert pulled it out. It was the obituary page. One obituary was circled in red. We gasped. The obituary read, "Eugene Kunkle loving friend of many sadly passed away yesterday afternoon after a terrible accident. He is survived by three of his 'foster children' Gilbert, Simon and Aria. May he rest in paradise."

Our jaws dropped. We stood frozen staring out to the hills. I couldn't feel my body. A tear ran down my cheek and my throat tightened up. Mr. Kunkle is dead.

I stared out to the newly green rolling grass hills followed by the small town of Helmsley. The tears began coming very quickly once I heard Simon and Gilbert crying. My vision blurred. Out in the yard where Coraline's trees once were, stood a tall dark figure.

CPSIA information can be obtained at www.ICGtesting.com
Printed in the USA
LVOW08s2333040314

376016LV00001B/189/P